THE PUFFIN BOOK OF
FUNNY STORIES

Worn out

A PUFFIN BOOK

PUFFIN BOOKS

UK | USA | Canada | Ireland | Australia
India | New Zealand | South Africa

Puffin Books is part of the Penguin Random House group of companies
whose addresses can be found at global.penguinrandomhouse.com.

www.penguin.co.uk
www.puffin.co.uk
www.ladybird.co.uk

Penguin
Random House
UK

First published 2021

001

The acknowledgements on p.211-213 constitute an
extension of this copyright page

The moral right of the contributors has been asserted

Set in 10.5/15.5pt Sabon LT Std
Typeset by Jouve (UK), Milton Keynes
Printed and bound in Great Britain by Clays Ltd, Elcograf S.p.A.

The authorized representative in the EEA is Penguin Random House Ireland,
Morrison Chambers, 32 Nassau Street, Dublin D02 YH68

A CIP catalogue record for this book is available from the British Library

ISBN: 978-0-241-43473-4

All correspondence to:
Puffin Books
Penguin Random House
One Embassy Gardens,
8 Viaduct Gardens,
London, SW11 7BW

Contents

Arabel's Birthday

from *More Arabel and Mortimer*

by Joan Aiken

Illustrated by Quentin Blake

*Arabel Jones has a mischievous raven called
Mortimer who causes havoc wherever he goes.
But he is also Arabel's best friend and she wouldn't
swap him for the world.*

THERE WERE visitors at Number Six, Rainwater Crescent. Mr Jones's cousin Gladys Line had come up to London to have a lot of special work done on her teeth at Rumbury Dental Hospital. This was going to take several days, so she was staying in Rainwater Crescent for a week. Her husband, Ray Line, who owned his own removal firm, had driven her down from Benwick-on-Tavey, where the Lines lived, along with two huge suitcases full of clothes, and their daughter Annie, who was just Arabel's age. Ray left his wife and daughter with the Joneses, and then drove up north again with a load of brass fire-tongs, two mahogany tables, and a love seat.

Just because somebody is the same age as you does not always mean that you are fond of them, and Arabel was not very fond of her cousin Annie, who had platinum blonde curls, and eyes the colour of curried beans, and a little squeaking whiny breathless voice in which she was always saying things that had better not have been said.

'Mummy, I saw Uncle Ben dip his finger in his soup to see if it was hot – that's not very nice, is it? Ooh, Mummy, Arabel put a HUGE spoonful of jam on her bread. Mummy, Aunt Martha's porridge isn't as good as yours, she doesn't put treacle and raisins in it. Mummy, Uncle Ben gave Arabel a much longer push on the swing than he did me, it's not *fair*. Mummy, Arabel's got slippers like rabbits and I haven't, it's not *fair*.'

Many things happened to Annie that were not fair; or she thought they were not; other people had different opinions.

'Ask me, that child ought to have been parcelled up at birth and posted off to Pernambuco,' said Mr Jones. He said this quietly to his wife in the garden, where he thought no one else could hear, but little Annie was sitting under the wheelbarrow, and she scrambled out and ran indoors to her mother, asking, 'Mummy, Mummy, why does Uncle Ben say I ought to have been posted to Pernambuco, where is Pernambuco, Mummy?'

'Ooo werp oh oo arhing ee ey hing ush ow,' said Annie's mother, who had just come back after a day spent at the dental hospital.

Annie had brought a great many of her own toys with her in the removal van, to prevent her becoming bored at Number Six, Rainwater Crescent while Cousin Gladys was at the hospital having her teeth fixed. The things that Annie had brought were much more expensive and complicated than Arabel's toys: there was computer golf, and an electronic exercise bicycle, and some radio-controlled tiddlywinks, a centrally-heated doll's house, a small infra-red oven that really roasted, magnetic dominoes, a computer guitar that would make up its own music and play without your needing to do anything, a book that would read aloud when you opened it (but it always read the same story, which was rather boring), a skateboard that ran on solar energy, a chess set that played games against itself, and lots of other things besides.

A lot of these toys didn't seem to need humans at all.

Arabel thought they seemed as if they would prefer to play by themselves, without being bothered to include Annie and Arabel in what they were doing. And many of them were so complicated – with their plugs and cables and switches and instrument panels and control-boxes – that they needed Mr Jones, first to start them up, and then to stay around and keep an eye to make sure they didn't go wrong, heat up red-hot, run out of fuel, chop somebody's arm off, or roll away, tossing out sparks, through the front door and into Rainwater Crescent. Mr Jones soon became fed up with this. He became tired of Annie's voice squeaking, 'Uncle Ben! Come *quick*! The doll's house is overheating again. The infra-red oven's letting off its warning whistle. Uncle *Ben*!'

Mr Jones said he had better things to do – such as driving his taxi – than sit all day keeping an eye on radio-controlled tiddlywinks. And, when the computer guitar had given Arabel quite a bad electric shock, Mr Jones carted a whole lot of Annie's toys up to the attic, and locked them away, despite her grumbles.

'They can't do any harm there,' he said. 'Besides, *I'm* not going to replace them, if they get broken while the kid's here. Those things probably cost a fortune. Let her play with them when she's back at home, and shock herself to death. Besides, if they're locked up, Mortimer can't get at them.'

This was true, even Annie could see. Mortimer, the Jones family raven, had, from the start, taken a huge amount of interest in Annie's toys; his black eyes sparkled bright as jet beads when first one glittering complicated object and then another was carried into the house by Cousin Ray Line.

Mortimer would dearly have liked to swallow the radioactive building bricks and squeeze inside the centrally-heated doll's house and have a ride on the electronic bicycle, and look at his own bones through the X-ray box, and roast something in the infra-red oven; he looked very downcast and sulky when Mr Jones packed all these things in the attic, and locked the door, and slipped the key on to the ring that he always carried in his pocket.

'*Nevermore* . . .' muttered Mortimer to himself.

But he did not give up hope of getting into the attic. One day – when all the family were out . . .

One thing that Mr Jones did not lock away, for she would not let him, was little Annie Line's Winky Doll, Mabel. Annie insisted on keeping Mabel by her wherever she went. This creature was larger than Annie and Arabel – *much* larger than Mortimer; it could walk, and nod its head, and wink its eye, and dance, and shake hands, and skate (that is, if you put it on ice, and strapped skates on to its feet); and it could give a horrible smile, and put its finger to its lips, and whisper, '*Listen! I'll tell you a secret!*'

Then, if you leaned your ear close beside its mouth, it would whisper something into your ear.

Annie was always putting her ear beside the Winky Doll's mouth and listening to what it whispered. Then she would burst into loud giggles and say, 'Oooooh! Winky Doll's just told me EVER such an exciting secret, and I'm not going to tell it to YOO-OO!'

After a day or two of this, Arabel waited for a chance when her Cousin Annie was out in the garden, asking Mr Jones for the twentieth time to stop his digging and give her a push in the swing.

'Ooh, Uncle Ben, please push me, please, Uncle Ben, please, Uncle Ben!'

While this was happening, Arabel put her ear close to the Winky Doll's mouth, and pressed its whisper button. The Winky Doll winked like mad, and nodded its head ever so many times, but all that Arabel actually managed to hear was 'Gabble-gabble-gabble-gabble, rhubarb-rhubarb-rhubarb'.

This was quite disappointing.

Perhaps the Winky Doll won't whisper for me because I'm not its proper owner, Arabel thought.

Or perhaps it never does whisper a real secret.

Mortimer the raven had taken a strong dislike to the Winky Doll from the very start. He hated the knowing smile on its fat face, and he hated the way it winked its eye and nodded its head. He hated its clothes, which were checked cotton with a great many patches sewn on all over. He hated its blue rolling eyes and its fat pudgy hands, and worst of all he hated the way it whispered secrets to little Annie Line.

Mortimer could not stand being left out of anything. If secrets were being whispered, he wanted them whispered to *him*.

'*Kaaaark*,' he grumbled furiously, each time Annie said, 'Winky Doll's told me a secret and I'm not going to tell yoo-oo . . .'

'Never mind, Mortimer,' said Arabel, who quite sympathised with what Mortimer was feeling, '*I'll* tell *you* a secret,' and she whispered to him, 'Pa's making me a see-saw for my birthday.'

But Mortimer was not appeased by this news. For one thing, he already knew about the seesaw, because he had watched Mr Jones dig a deep hole, down at the far end of the garden, and sink a post in the hole, and set it in cement; and he had also spent some time in Mr Jones's garden shed workshop, while the hinge was being fitted on the seat part of the see-saw; until Mr Jones noticed that Mortimer had swallowed half a jarful of brass upholstery tacks, and requested him to leave.

The fifth day of Cousin Gladys's visit was Arabel's birthday. The see-saw had been finished, ready for use. As well as the see-saw, Arabel had been given, by her mother, a little marble pastryboard and rolling pin, also a small pudding basin, flour-sifter, wooden spoon and cheese-grater, so that she could make pastry or cheese straws if she wanted to. Mortimer the raven was very fond of cheese straws. From her father Arabel had a set of gardening tools, spade, fork, rake, hoe, watering can and wheelbarrow. Mortimer at once wanted a ride in the wheelbarrow, which was exactly the right size for him.

'I've bought you some tulip and daffodil bulbs too,' said Mr Jones. 'Otherwise, as it's October, there wouldn't be much you could plant. But you can put the bulbs in now, and then you'll see them come up in the spring.'

Arabel was very happy with her presents. She had also a toy dentist's set from Annie, a red handbag from Cousin Gladys, and, from Great-Uncle Arthur, a packet of six Mortimer bars.

Mortimer bars were a new kind of chocolate bar that had just been invented. They had layers of butterscotch, nuts, marzipan and crumbly biscuit, wrapped in a thick chocolate rind.

Arabel liked them because of the butterscotch, nuts and biscuit; Mortimer liked them because of the name. The name had nothing to do with Mortimer really; Fun-Folks Foods Ltd, the chocolate company who made the bars, had never heard of Mortimer. They chose the name because it began with an M, for they already had several other chocolate bars with M names, Monarch and Macho and Monster and Magpie (which was black and white chocolate). Now there were big posters all over London, especially in Underground stations, showing a frantic mother and her little boy who was howling with hunger. The caption underneath the picture said:

> She should have
> bought him a
> MORTIMER!

Mortimer was delighted with these posters, and let out a loud '*Kaaark*' of satisfaction whenever he saw his own name written up so large. (Mortimer was not able to read many words. But Arabel had taught him to recognise his own name when it was printed.)

Little Annie did not think highly of Arabel's presents.

'Who wants a crummy old *cooking set*?' she said. 'That's only for *babies*. And who wants to work in the *garden*? I'd sooner ride on my exercise bicycle. And as for those mingy chocolate bars . . . ! When it's *my* birthday, *my* Dad gives me a *huge* box of chocolates, five layers deep, that costs pounds and pounds and pounds; and I'm allowed to eat the chocolates till I'm sick.'

'Fine goings on, I must say,' said Mrs Jones.

'But with the Mortimer bars,' pointed out Arabel, 'you can win half a million pounds.'

Arabel was right about this. Fun-Folks Foods Ltd had launched their new chocolate bar with an advertising campaign that told the public: 'Save the wrappers from twenty different Mortimer bars, fit them together, and make yourself a map which will lead you to the exciting spot where a solid block of gold is buried worth £500,000! Five hundred thousand pounds!'

Every Mortimer bar had part of a map printed on the inside of its wrapper. When you had managed to collect the twenty different bits that made up the whole map, and stuck them all together in the right order, you had to solve the secret clues printed on the map, which told you where the gold was buried. It might be anywhere in the whole country. The map was dotted all over with little pictures of people and animals doing different things, and clues about these activities. 'Emus bury wart,' said one clue. 'Subway, Mr True?' said another. 'We may rub rust,' said another, and another said 'A rum ruby stew'.

Arabel and Mortimer had already collected more than twenty Mortimer bar wrappers. They had not actually eaten all that number of chocolate bars; but Mortimer was extremely sharp at spotting the gold, purple and brown wrappers on the pavement, or in litter bins, or on Rumbury Waste where he and Arabel sometimes went roller-skating.

Mrs Jones did not approve of Mortimer picking up the wrappers.

'They're sure to be covered in germs,' she said.

But Mortimer was very quick and clever at flipping them up with his beak and whipping them under his wing, and not bringing them out until he was back at home. He and Arabel had a wooden cigar box where they kept their collection of wrappers.

Some of the twenty wrappers that Arabel and Mortimer had saved were duplicates; they did not yet have a complete set of all that were needed. However, with Great-Uncle Arthur's six, there seemed a good chance that they might have the whole set.

'But you're not to go unwrapping and eating them all at once!' warned Mrs Jones. 'One a day – after dinner. You can cut each bar into three bits, one for each of you.'

Mortimer's eyes sparkled at this, but Annie said, 'That's not *fair*! That's *mean*! *My* Mum lets me eat a whole bar whenever I want to, *and* as many chocolates as I like.'

'Yes, and look at your spotty face,' said Mrs Jones, but she said this to herself, not aloud, for she did not want to be unkind to a guest. Not that Annie took any pains to be kind to the Jones family. She pinched Arabel to make her get off the swing, poked Mortimer with her doll's parasol, told Mr Jones that his face was too red, and grumbled because Mrs Jones did not have ice cream at every meal.

Arabel's birthday, a Saturday, was fine and sunny, so she went into the garden directly after breakfast to plant her new bulbs with her new gardening tools. Annie didn't want to be left out of this, although she despised gardening, so Arabel let her have half the bulbs, and take turns with the spade, trowel and rake, which were red, with yellow handles.

Mortimer preferred to dig holes with his beak.

'Perhaps we'll find the gold Mortimer bar, if we dig enough holes,' said Annie. 'It might be in this garden as well as anywhere,' and she began digging holes all over Mr Jones's garden beds, until he came out of his work-shed and stopped her.

When they had planted all the bulbs (Annie planted hers upside down, because she said that way they would grow downwards and come up in Australia; Arabel was not very happy about this), they played on the new see-saw.

Annie and Arabel were just about the same height and weight; they found they could use the see-saw very well together.

Mortimer did not like being left out. He jumped up and down with annoyance, and shouted '*Nevermore!*' so many times that neighbours in gardens on each side began to complain.

'That bird is a pest,' they said. 'There's never any peace while he's around.'

'He wants a turn on the see-saw,' said Arabel.

'Well, give him one, for mercy's sake!' said Mr Cross next door.

'He can't have *my* place,' said Annie.

'Come on, Mortimer, you can sit on my end,' said Arabel, and she got off and lifted Mortimer on to her seat. Mr Jones had set in crossbars for a handhold; Mortimer clutched the crossbar with his claw.

Unfortunately he was far too heavy for Annie on the see-saw; Mortimer had recently swallowed an iron wedge, a claw hammer and an old metal doorstop, in Mr Jones's workroom; and when he sat on the see-saw, the other end, with Annie on it, shot up into the air and stayed there.

'Oooooh! I'm slipping! Let me down!' shrieked Annie, high up on her end of the see-saw.

Mortimer flopped off his end, and Annie came down with a bump.

'What a shame,' said Arabel. 'Let's try with both of us on one seat and Mortimer on the other.'

But even so, he was too heavy for them.

'You've been eating too much, you fat old pig of a rook!' said Annie rudely. 'Come on, Arabel, let's play dressing-up.'

Mortimer was offended, and also disappointed, because he had been looking forward to a turn on the see-saw. He ruffled out all his feathers, went into a sulk, and walked away to watch Mr Jones, who was burning up dead cabbage stalks and thorn twigs in the garden incinerator, along with the chips of wood left over from the see-saw.

Mortimer watched Mr Jones with great attention. Then he began bringing things to be burned; first he fetched some sticks, but Mr Jones

said they were his pea-sticks and were being saved for next year; next Mortimer found the cardboard box that had had the bulbs in it, which Mr Jones let him burn; then he brought the paper wrappings from Arabel's tool set, and a whole tangle of garden raffia that had gone rotten, so Mr Jones let him burn those things too.

'Now that's enough, Mortimer,' said Mr Jones at this point. 'I've got other things to do than watch a raven burning rubbish. You run along and play with the girls.'

Mr Jones went off to drive his taxi.

Mortimer never ran anywhere. He walked away slowly, with his head sunk in his neck-feathers.

The girls were in Arabel's room, dressing up in each other's clothes. Little Annie had brought from home an enormous suitcase full of dresses and pinafores and skirts and sweaters and jeans and shirts, all clean and new; she could have changed everything she had on, from the skin up, five times a day and still have had some things left over by the end of the visit. So Arabel was having quite an exciting time trying on her cousin's wardrobe. Unluckily Arabel herself did not have nearly so many clothes, and also she was thinner and a little shorter than Annie; Mrs Jones had made her a new blue dress for her birthday but when Annie tried it on, she tore it at the neck.

'Your clothes are boring,' said Annie. 'Let's dress up in Auntie Martha's clothes and play Kings and Queens.'

Without asking permission, Annie got Mrs Jones's fur coat out of the black plastic mothproof satchel where it lived, and put it on; then she made herself a crown from an empty ice-cream container cut into spikes.

When Mortimer discovered what the girls were doing, he was not interested. He had not the least wish to play Kings and Queens. He tried to get into the black plastic satchel where Mrs Jones's fur coat had been kept, which he had always wanted to do, but Arabel would not let him. So, while Arabel was making herself a crown out of three egg-boxes stuck together, Mortimer went grumpily downstairs again. On the way up he had noticed the Winky Doll arranged in an armchair in the lounge, staring at the blank television screen. (Annie had left the TV switched on for the Winky Doll, but Mrs Jones had switched it off, muttering 'Dolls watching telly, what next?' before going back to her kitchen work.)

Mrs Jones was busy making Arabel's birthday cake.

Mortimer went into the lounge and tried to pick up the Winky Doll. But, although he was very strong, the doll was too floppy and bulky and awkward for him to carry.

'*Nevermore!*' he croaked to himself.

The Winky Doll's hands and feet were too fat and shiny for Mortimer's beak or claws to grasp them. At length he managed to drag the doll off the chair and on to the floor by its skirt; then he began hauling it across the floor by its hair. Some hair came out. And Mortimer knocked over a small table and a standard lamp.

At the sound of the table falling, Mrs Jones called, 'Arabel and Annie, what are you doing?'

'We aren't doing *anything*, Auntie Martha,' called Annie from upstairs. Mrs Jones went to see what this meant. She was very annoyed at finding Annie in her fur coat.

'*That goes straight* back in its satchel, and don't let me see you touch it again,' she said. 'And you'd better tidy up all this mess. What Cousin Gladys will say when she sees all Annie's nice new things crumpled up like that, I *do* not know.'

'Oo werp oh oo arhing ee ey hing ush ow,' was all that Gladys Line actually said when she came back from the dental hospital, but by that time, of course, the clothes had been folded up and put back in Annie's drawer.

Mrs Jones was even more annoyed when she found that Arabel's new blue dress had been torn at the neck.

'You girls go and play *outside*,' said Mrs Jones, and she went back, with her lips pressed tight together, to the kitchen, to see how Arabel's birthday cake was getting on. The girls played radio-controlled tiddlywinks on the back doorstep.

While Mrs Jones was upstairs, Mortimer had managed to drag the Winky Doll through the kitchen, out of the back door, and down the sloping cement path to the garden incinerator behind the laurel bush. He propped the doll against the side of the incinerator and rested for a moment or two; all that dragging had been hard work. Then he flapped himself up and perched on the rim of the incinerator. Then he leaned down and took a good hold of the doll's hair with his beak.

Then, with one terrific jerk, twitch, flap, hoist and scramble, he wrenched up the Winky Doll, hauled it over the rim of the incinerator, and dropped it down inside.

There were still some glowing ends of twigs and slivers of wood smouldering away under the ashes at the bottom of the pile of burnt garden rubbish. When the Winky Doll had stood on its head in the ashes for a few minutes, the dry blonde hair began to burn; then, with a little spurt of flame, the frilly collar caught fire.

'Kaaark!' said Mortimer, delighted; and he flopped off the rim of the incinerator (which was rather too close to the flames for comfort) and watched from the handle of Mr Jones's wheelbarrow, as, with a fluttering roaring sound, the Winky Doll burned up completely. A thick black column of smoke rose up from the foam rubber with which the doll was stuffed. Quite soon there was nothing left in the bottom of the incinerator but a squirmy coil of shiny greasy black brittle stuff.

'Nevermore!' said Mortimer with deep satisfaction, and he went away to sit on the bottom end of the see-saw, and think about Mortimer bars, and milk chocolate, and mince pies, and mushrooms, and all the other things he liked to eat.

'Girls,' said Mrs Jones presently, seeing them on the back step, 'it'll be teatime soon, why don't you take a bit of exercise before tea, instead of just sitting there?'

Arabel and Annie stood up. If Arabel had been on her own, she would have found plenty to do in the garden: sweeping up leaves, picking bunches of Michaelmas daisies to put in meat-paste jars, collecting empty snail shells, and looking for nuts in the hazel hedge behind Mr Jones's work-shed. But Annie did not want to do any of those things; she said they were boring.

'Let's get out the garden hose and water your bulbs that we planted,' Annie said.

'Pa doesn't like me to get out the hose,' Arabel said doubtfully.

'Well he's not here,' said Annie, and she dragged out the hose, which was long and green and shiny, and lived in the shed, wound up on a kind of wheel.

Annie unwound a whole lot of the hose. Then she fitted the end of it over the garden tap and turned the tap on.

Annie had left the nozzle of the hose pointing towards Arabel, who was walking slowly towards Mortimer, still sitting on the see-saw; when Annie turned the tap full on, a sharp jet of water burst out of the hose nozzle and drenched Arabel from head to foot.

'Eeeech!' cried Arabel, in surprise; and Mortimer, who had climbed off the see-saw and started walking towards her, stopped short and gazed in astonishment. Next minute he got soused as well, for Annie, almost doubled up with laughter, grabbed the nozzle and turned it in Mortimer's direction.

Mortimer did not in the least mind being sprayed with water; his coat of black feathers was so thick and waterproof that most of the spray just ran off on to the grass. But he was very anxious to get a closer look at the hose; this was because, whenever Mr Jones used it for watering the garden, he forbade Mortimer to come anywhere near, and, indeed, generally shut the raven inside the house while watering was being done. 'For you know what would happen,' he said. 'That black monster would eat up the hose like spaghetti before you could say Columbus!'

So Mortimer had never been able to get a close look at the hose, and now he was not going to waste his chance. He thought the hose looked as if it might be made of liquorice.

Just then Mrs Jones came out with a couple of teacloths to hang on the line.

'Girls!' she called. 'It's just going to be teatime. Birthday cake! Where are you?'

Then she saw Arabel, soaked from head to foot, with her fair hair hanging plastered all round her like a yellow shawl, and the water streaming off her wet dress.

'*Arabel Jones!* What*ever* have you been *doing*?'

'Look out, Auntie Martha!' squeaked Annie in fits of giggles. 'Or I'll turn the hose on you too!'

But at that moment Mortimer, who had been observing the length of shiny green hosepipe very attentively, walked along it towards Annie, giving it, as he went, a series of brisk sharp stabs with his beak – just the way a cook cuts with a knife round the rim of a pastry tart – peck, peck, peck, peck, peck! At each peck along the pipe, out shot a jet of water. And the last one hit little Annie Line, and drenched her as thoroughly as her cousin.

Mrs Jones, lips jammed together to stop her saying something she might later regret, went and turned off the garden tap. Then she jerked the lever that coiled the hosepipe, and rewound it on to its wheel. Then she locked up the hose in the garden shed and pocketed the key.

'Just you wait till your father hears about this!' she said to Arabel. 'Go along – indoors, the pair of you, and get out of those wet things.'

'Shan't you let us have Arabel's birthday cake now?' pertly asked Annie Line, turning to stare at Mrs Jones with her curried-bean eyes, as she slowly dripped her way upstairs, all over Mrs Jones's pale green stair carpet.

Annie was used to being in disgrace, which was a daily event with her at home; disgrace never lasted long in her family.

'We'll see,' said Mrs Jones grimly, following Arabel into the bathroom with a towel.

However when Mr Jones came home, which he soon did, for he had promised to be back in time for Arabel's birthday tea, he said, after hearing the story, 'Well, Martha, it wasn't Arabel's fault – for it was Annie's idea to play with the hose. So I don't see why Arabel shouldn't have her birthday cake. And as for

Mortimer, it's no more than you'd expect of *him*.'

'It's all that perishing little Annie – I could wring her neck,' muttered Mrs Jones. 'Nothing but trouble since she's been in the house. Normally our Arabel's good as gold – and Mortimer at least is just himself, that's all you can say of him.'

'Well, Annie's a visitor, you can't punish the child,' said Ben, 'and thank goodness she and Gladys are going on Monday; nothing too bad can happen between now and then,' he added hopefully. 'Let's go on and have the birthday tea, Martha.'

So they had the birthday tea, in the kitchen, with a pink tablecloth over the big kitchen table, and candles on the pink cake, and Annie and Arabel rather clean and quiet, and Mortimer decidedly overexcited, swallowing the crackers as fast as they were pulled, sometimes even before they were pulled, as well as all the things that came out of them, riddles and whistles and rings and paper caps and plastic flowers.

Cousin Gladys returned from her day's treatment at the hospital and swallowed a cup of tea, but was unable to eat anything because of her teeth.

'Ooo werp oh oo arhing ee ey hing ush ow,' she said. 'Ahhy irhy, Arel eerie.'

Later it was bedtime for the girls, and Annie began looking for her Winky Doll.

'That's funny. I thought I left her in the lounge,' she said. 'I thought I left her in the armchair watching *Racing at Windsor*.'

'So you did, but I came in and switched off the programme. Wasting television on dolls, indeed!' said Mrs Jones.

'Did you put my Winky Doll away somewhere, Aunt Martha?'

'Didn't touch the object,' said Mrs Jones.

'Somebody knocked over the table and the light, and broke the bulb,' said Mr Jones, taking the broken bulb out of the standard lamp. 'Was that you girls?'

They shook their heads.

Then Arabel noticed a button from the Winky Doll's dress lying on the carpet near the door. Just one button. And a tuft of hair.

A sudden awful thought came into her head.

'Mortimer,' she said. 'Did you take Annie's Winky Doll anywhere?'

'*Kaaark*,' said Mortimer dreamily.

'Mortimer. Where did you take the Winky Doll?'

Without the least hesitation, Mortimer proudly led the way to the garden incinerator. By now it was dark, they had to switch on the light outside the back door, and carry torches with them to shine on what Mortimer had to show them – which was a pile of ash. There was one brass button left among the ashes, and a blue eye.

'MORTIMER!!!'

Little Annie Line went into whooping hysterics, and had to be given hot milk with sherry and treacle in it.

'My Winky Doll!' she wept and hiccuped. 'My Winky Doll! She knew all those secrets – and – and now she'll never tell them to me any more!'

'Not a bad thing that, if you ask me,' muttered Mr Jones to himself. But to Cousin Gladys he said, 'Of course we'll replace the blas – the doll, Gladys – as it was our raven that did the damage.'

'She was the only one who told me secrets!' wailed Annie.

'Ah, oo, Ben,' said Gladys Line.

'I don't want any other doll!' screamed Annie. 'I want my Whispering Winky! Just let me get at that Mortimer! I'll roast him in my infra-red oven!'

'Kaaark,' said Mortimer.

'I'll bath him in a bowl of bleach and turn him white!'

'Kaaark.'

'I'll stand him on his head in the blender and liquidize him.'

'Kaaark.'

'I'll stick him in the deep-freeze and turn him to a block of frozen raven.'

'Kaaark. Kaaark.'

'I'll chop him into drumsticks with Dad's electric carving knife –'

'Ow, Annie! Oo erp oh oo arhing ee ey hing ush, ow,' said her mother.

'*I* believe that child's got a temperature,' said Mrs Jones. 'She'd better take a couple of Easydorm tablets, and stay in bed tomorrow.'

To her husband later Mrs Jones said, 'All those wicked things she was saying she'd like to do to our Mortimer, the spoilt little madam! Why, I'm half scared of what she might try, if she had a chance to get at him. I'll keep her in bed tomorrow, out of harm's way, while Gladys has her last treatment.'

'Just the same, I'd back Mortimer, if it came to it,' said Mr Jones. 'I reckon he can take care of himself.'

'I dunno, Ben. The look in that child's eye! She really had me scared.'

Next day the travel plans of Gladys and Annie were upset by a telephone call from Annie's teenage brother Dick, to say that Ray Line had been involved in a motorway pile-up, and was in Benwick hospital with a busted collarbone, and his van, full of plastic draining boards, was a write-off.

'Poor Gladys is *ever* so upset,' said Mrs Jones, telling her husband about this when he came home from taxi-driving. 'Now she's got to go home by train, and she says she doesn't know if she can face the journey, on her own, with Annie and all that luggage they brought. So I said I'd go to Benwick with her, and stay till Ray comes out of hospital – though it'll mean taking Arabel as well. I thought I'd leave Mortimer with you, Ben.'

'No. No. No!' said Mr Jones. 'Can't have that bird on his own in the house whenever I go out on a job, or round the corner for a pint. He'll have to travel along with you.'

'Oh, Ben! I'd never manage all that *and* Mortimer.'

'Then I'll have to come along on the train,' said Mr Jones. 'See you to Benwick, put you all in a cab, then get the next train back to London. Can't use my taxi, the clutch wants fixing. It'd never get us to Newcastle.'

'Oh, Ben! *Could* you? That's ever so thoughtful of you.'

Cousin Gladys thought so too. 'Ah, oo, Ben – ah eyer oh ay och oo!'

But difficulties arose, and this plan almost got nipped in the bud, when Cousin Gladys and little Annie began seriously getting down to their packing. For everybody except little Annie had forgotten about the things in the loft – the exercise bicycle, the computer golf, the mechanised ping-pong, toy infra-red oven, do-it-yourself X-ray kit, rubber dinghy, and a huge box of fireworks which Cousin Gladys had bought on her way back from the hospital one day because it would be Guy Fawkes soon.

'Can't take all *that* load,' said Mr Jones firmly. 'We'd need a spare guard's van all to ourselves. No – those things'll have to stay here till Ray gets his collarbone mended and his van replaced and comes to fetch them.'

Since he was being so kind about travelling to Benwick with her, Cousin Gladys could not object to this, but little Annie was highly indignant.

'Leave all my lovely toys behind for that horrible bird to burn up? Not likely!'

'Oh, Annie! Ooo werp oh oo arhing eee ey hing!'

Annie stuck out her lip and scowled horribly. But Mr Jones gave her such a quelling look that she turned quite pale and muttered, 'Well, we've *got* to take the fireworks. There wouldn't be any *point* to the fireworks, if we didn't have them for Guy Fawkes.'

Finally the luggage was all packed and collected together – Arabel and Mrs Jones's moderate-sized bags, to last them for a few days at Benwick, and Mrs Jones's fur coat in its black plastic satchel – 'What d'you want to take your fur coat for, Martha?' demanded Mr Jones. 'You won't be doing anything posh in Benwick.'

'It'll be cold up north, Ben. Besides, burglars might come here, while we're away, and steal it.'

'Well, why not wear it then, instead of carrying it in that bag?'

'Wear my *fur coat* on the *train*? Are you crazy, Ben Jones?'

Then there was a huge pork pie in a plastic container inside a rucksack, which Mrs Jones had made so no one would have to cook when they got to Cousin Gladys's house. And there was another rucksack with a picnic in it, to eat on the four-hour train journey. And there was Mortimer in his travel basket lined with an old pink blanket that had been Arabel's cot cover when she was smaller. There were Annie's and Gladys's enormous cases of clothes and the box of fireworks, which Annie had insisted on taking – besides another bag containing her radio-controlled tiddlywinks, magnetic dominoes, self-play chess set and solar-powered skateboard. All these things were jumbled together at the foot of the stairs.

'Blimey,' muttered Mr Jones. 'We don't need a taxi to take us to King's Cross – we need the Royal Coach.'

Mr Jones's friend Sid Ivy was driving them to the station.

Just as they had half the luggage out on the pavement, a police car pulled up alongside.

'You going away, Ben?' called Sergeant Pike, who was a friend of the Jones family.

'Martha and the kid are,' said Mr Jones. 'I'll be back tonight. Why?'

'Oh, if you're coming back, that's OK. We're keeping a sharp eye on all unoccupied property round here just now. The Rumbury Rakes are out of jail, and they've had to shift out of the Palindrome because it's being pulled down.'

'What's the Palindrome?' Annie asked.

'It's the old empty cinema opposite Rumbury Market.'

'Who are the Rumbury Rakes?'

'The Rumbury Rakes are a gang of very dangerous criminals, young lady,' said Sergeant Pike. 'You'd better be thankful you don't have anything to do with them.'

'Oh, Ben!' said Mrs Jones fearfully. 'Are you sure it's all right to go off and leave our house empty?'

'Don't be soft, Martha, of course it is. Sergeant Pike here will keep an eye on it, won't you, Jim?' said Mr Jones impatiently. 'Come on, come on, at this rate we'll miss the ten-thirty and maybe young Dick'll be there on the platform at Benwick wondering where we've got to. Hurry up, you kids, get some of that stuff loaded into the cab.'

Everybody began dashing to and fro across the pavement, bumping into other people, tripping over things that other people had just put down, getting in each other's way, asking questions to everybody else and telling them what not to do.

'Where's the pork pie? Gladys, did you put in the toys?'

'Arabel! What have you done with the picnic?'

'Ben! You can't put those fireworks on top of my fur coat! Suppose they were to go off!'

From all the hurrying and scurrying, and the amount of luggage that was being shifted, anyone watching might have thought that the Jones family were leaving for a six-month trip to the Seychelles. At last they were all jammed in the cab, the two mothers on the back seat, with Annie between them, Arabel and Mr Jones on the tip-up seats travelling backwards. Annie was in a sulk because *she* wanted to be on a tip-up seat. Arabel was worried because Mortimer's travel basket was in the boot instead of on her lap. That was because Annie had flatly refused to travel in a car with the raven.

'If I have to be as close to him as that, I'll scream and scream till I'm sick. I *hate* that bird!'

'She'll *have* to go with him in the train,' said Mr Jones grimly.

But his wife whispered to him, 'Hush! Gladys gave Annie one of my Easydorm tablets in her breakfast cereal. She'll soon quiet down, go to sleep most likely. And *I* gave a tablet to Mortimer in one of my ginger-and-marmalade tarts. I reckon he'll sleep all the way to Benwick.'

'That was smart of you, Martha,' said Mr Jones, who knew how partial Mortimer was to ginger-and-marmalade tarts. 'Maybe, after all, we'll have a bit of peace and quiet on the trip.'

What they didn't know was that Annie had snatched Mortimer's marmalade tart while he was looking hopefully at Mrs Jones's black fur coat satchel as it sat on the bottom step of the stairs.

Somehow they all managed to get themselves unloaded from the taxi at King's Cross, and on to the nonstop InterCity train to Benwick-on-Tavey.

Mr Jones piled all the luggage into the racks – including Mortimer's raven-basket. He failed to notice that the basket did not seem quite so heavy as it should have been.

'Will Mortimer be all right up there in the rack, Pa?' Arabel asked anxiously.

'He'll soon let us know if he's not,' said her father. 'You can rely on Mortimer for that.'

Arabel nodded. She knew this was true. Mortimer would soon begin to shout and carry on if he wasn't happy. In any case he knew how to undo the lid of his basket.

After Arabel had looked out of the window for a while, at the flat country north of King's Cross, she took out the drawing-book she had brought with her, and the old cigar box full of Mortimer bar wrappers, and settled down to working out how they should be fitted together. They were on the kind of train that had tables between the seats, so Arabel could do this job comfortably on the table.

Annie grumbled terribly at first, because Mr Jones had not bought her a comic, because her magnetic dominoes were at the bottom of a case full of clothes and she was not allowed to unpack it, because the buffet car was not open yet and she and Arabel could not go and buy packets of crisps and cans of Thirst-Aid; but then, just as Mr Jones was muttering that he knew what *he'd* do with a young 'un that went on so, she fell into a deep sleep that lasted till past Newcastle and the end of the picnic lunch.

Meanwhile Arabel, all excited after several hours of hard thinking, cried out, 'Pa! *Pa!* I believe I've put this together right! Look! It all fits! And, look, all these clues – "A rum ruby stew", and "Wary Emu burst", and "Subway, Mr True?" – if you move the letters about into a different order, they all spell the same thing!'

'And what's that?' asked Mr Jones, yawning, for he had eaten two thick ham sandwiches and a large heavy piece of coconut cake. 'Ask *me*, all these competitions do is get you to pay out more money.'

'No, no, Pa, if you win this one you dig up a gold bar that's worth five hundred thousand pounds! And it's all because Mortimer has worked so hard collecting wrappers – I ought to get him down and tell him –'

'No, no, he's asleep, thank goodness, leave him be. So what do the clues spell then?'

'They all spell RUMBURY WASTE! And I believe that's where the gold bar's buried!'

'Eh? What?' said Mr Jones, suddenly alert after all, and he took the maps all made out of Mortimer bar wrappers which Arabel had carefully stuck together. It was a copy of a regular Ordnance Survey map, but the place names had been blanked out so there were just paths and brooks and hills and copses and pylons and parish boundaries marked, and a bit of red road running along one side.

'Sure, that's Rumbury Waste,' said Mr Jones, after carefully studying the map. 'I drive past it

forty times a week, I ought to know. There's the water tower. There's the sewage farm. There's the Public Conveniences, there's the allotments. What gave you the idea, Arabel, lovey? My word, I believe you've gone and won us all that money! What do we have to do?'

'Phone that telephone number at the top of the map,' said Arabel, all excited. 'Give your name and the answer. And they'll give you the last clue, where to dig. You'd better do it from Benwick Station, Pa, as soon as we get there, in case someone else has thought of the answer too.'

Arabel's voice was joyful. If we win that money, she was thinking, it will pay for a horrible new Winky Doll for Annie, and a new hose for Pa; it isn't fair that he should have to pay for those things.

By now the train was running alongside the River Tavey, about to enter Benwick.

'Ay, uh, Annie,' said her mother. Annie, who had fallen asleep again after lunch, yawned and stretched and grumbled. 'We never had any *tea*. I wanted to have tea in the buffet car.'

Everyone began standing up, and bumping into everybody else, putting books and magazines and knitting and sweet papers into bags and cases. The train sighed to a stop and the automatic doors opened.

'Oh look – there's Auntie Clotilda!' yelled Annie joyfully. 'And Uncle Swen! Perhaps they'll take us out to tea at Scotswood's!'

She jumped out of the train shouting, 'Auntie Clotilda, Arabel's horrible old raven burned my Winky Doll! Wasn't he horrible?'

'Burned up your dolly? Oh, you poor little love,' cried Auntie Clotilda, who was big and round and pink with yellow hair, and looked like the sort of thing you win at a fair by shooting six glass bottles with an air gun. Uncle Swen was small and fat and red-faced with glasses, and he put in a 'Huff!' before everything he said, in order to make sure that everybody was listening.

'Uncle Swen will buy you another dolly, you poor little mite, won't you, Swen?' said Auntie Clotilda. 'We've come to stay with your Mum till she's better.'

'Huff! Buy the girlie another doll if she wants it,' said Uncle Swen. 'Mind you – huff! – never thought she cared for it all that much; never took any notice of it that *I* ever saw.'

'Oh, sweetheart, of course she did – she loved every hair on its head – pleased to meet you dear,

I'm sure,' said Auntie Clotilda, who had not met Mrs Jones before, and then she and Uncle Swen began bustling about, helping to get all the luggage out of the train, while Mr Jones, seeing there was plenty of assistance, bolted away to find a telephone and ring up Fun-Folks Foods. Annie's brother Dick was there on the platform too; he had platinum hair like his sister, all curls, and a lot of teeth that stuck out, and red sunglasses, so that he looked like a white rat wearing a corduroy jacket. He gave Arabel a superior glance, but did not speak to her. Having taken all the luggage out, he and Uncle Swen began shifting it across the platform towards the exit. 'What a lot of stuff,' said Uncle Swen. 'Anyone 'ud think you'd been away for a year, Gladys.'

Arabel, who had been rather silent and shy at meeting all these new people, suddenly said, 'Oh, mind out, please! That's my raven – in the wicker basket.'

'What?' said Auntie Clotilda with a screech. 'You brought that *raven*? The one that ate Annie's Winky Doll? I'm not having that thing under the same roof with me. Our poor little Peke-a-Boo would have a heart attack at the sight of the nasty bird!'

'Huff! Quite agree!' said Uncle Swen. 'Dangerous, nasty things. Give you citykosis as soon as look at you.'

'He didn't eat the Winky Doll, Aunt Clotilda, he burned it up,' said Arabel politely.

'Well, I'm sure!' said Mrs Jones, quite affronted – in spite of the fact that, when at home, she had plenty of hard things to say about Mortimer. 'I'm sure *we've* no wish to push ourselves in where our raven's not welcome! Seeing as how you have got your brother and sister-in-law to look after you, Gladys, Arabel and I may as well travel straight back to London with Ben –'

'Huff! Best put the bird in the luggage locker till it's time for your train back,' said Uncle Swen.

'Oh, please, no!' cried Arabel in horror; she was sure that Mortimer would hate to wake up from his nap and find that his travel basket was packed inside a left-luggage locker.

'Oo'll ay aha uhuh o ee ehore oo oh, Arha?' said Gladys, rather unhappy at the way the Jones family were being treated.

Mrs Jones glanced at the station clock and murmured to Arabel, 'It'll only be for an hour or so, lovey. Dad was going to get the four o'clock back –' and while she was still speaking, Annie and Dick had grabbed various bits of the Joneses' luggage and raced off, giggling, towards the luggage lockers, which were in a big silvery bank along one wall of the station. 'Mind my fur coat – it's in the black satchel –' Mrs Jones called after them anxiously. 'Mind the picnic basket, it's got breakables in it!' 'Mind Mortimer!' called Arabel, even more anxiously. She started to run after them. Uncle Swen and Aunt Clotilda had bundled Cousin Gladys into a plum-coloured Ford Festina, calling, 'You others come in a cab. We'll have a cup of tea waiting for you!' and they drove away.

At that moment Mr Jones reappeared, looking white and wild-eyed.

'What is it, Pa, what's the matter?' cried Arabel. She stopped chasing Dick and Annie. 'Couldn't you get through to Fun-Folks Foods?'

'Get through?' said Mr Jones. 'Get through? Oh yes, I got *through* all right.'

Absently he took the key of the left-luggage locker that Dick Line handed him – it had a thick red round plastic disc on it, the size of a marshmallow, with a number. Mr Jones put the key in his pocket.

'Ben? What *is* it?' wailed Mrs Jones fearfully. 'What's the matter? Why do you look so all-overish?'

'I got through to Fun-Folks Foods,' said Mr Jones, 'and they told me –'

'Oh, Pa,' cried Arabel, guessing, 'has somebody else already –'

'Yes, they have! And who do you think phoned in with the right answer?'

'I can't guess, Pa. Somebody we know? Somebody nice?'

'It's that pack of hoodlums that call themselves the Rumbury Rakes,' said Mr Jones. 'The man at Fun-Folks Foods told me that. He said I was the second person to come up with the correct solution. Fork O'Farrell, the leader of the Rumbury Rakes, phoned in at half-past seven this morning, and they were out on Rumbury Waste, digging up the gold bar, at eight.'

'Oh, Pa! What a shame!'

If Annie hadn't been staying with us, thought Arabel, I'd have had more time to work on that puzzle. I'd have finished it days ago.

But Mr Jones hadn't finished.

'And where do you think the gang are *now*?' he said to his wife.

'Oh, Ben! They're not at *our* –'

'That's right! The cops spotted them on Rumbury Waste and chased them in a police car – they're wanted for smuggling – and now they're holed up in Number Six, Rainwater Crescent. Is there a train back before the four o'clock?' he asked Dick Line. 'If so, I'm getting it.'

'Oh, *Ben*! You mean that pack of young monsters is in *our* home, using *our* soap and towels and eating my Fruity Crumble Cake?'

'They're eating it if they've got time,' growled Mr Jones. 'Half the cops in North London are sitting round the house, the Fun-Folks Foods feller told me, with smoke jets and pepper-guns and sneezing-powder sprays –'

'Oh! My clean loose covers!' wailed Mrs Jones. 'And the new bathroom lino, and twenty pounds you just spent on having the back door glass mended –' Then she thought a minute, and said, 'There! You see I was *right* to bring my fur coat, and I'm glad I did.'

'Where is it?' asked Mr Jones, looking round at the iron pillars and arches of Benwick Station. 'Where are our things?'

Just as they were starting to explain to Mr Jones that, owing to the arrival of Uncle Swen and Auntie

Clotilda they were not now needed at the Lines' house, and planned to return to London with him, a very loud voice began announcing something over the station public address system.

'ATTENTION! Attention! Attention! We have reason to believe that a dangerous article, possibly explosive, has been deposited in one of the left-luggage lockers. We must ask all passengers to leave the station at once, in an orderly manner. If you are catching a train, get into it, and it will go. Otherwise, please leave by one of the exits into Rosburgh Road, Glenside Road, or Motherwell Road, where you will be kept informed of events by the police. We repeat: please leave the station in an orderly manner as fast as possible.'

'Oh, Pa,' cried Arabel in dismay. 'We *can't* leave the station! Mortimer's in one of the left-luggage lockers. Annie and Dick put him there before I could stop them – along with Ma's fur coat and our luggage and the picnic bag.'

'Ohmygawd!' exclaimed Mr Jones. He pulled the red-tagged key out of his pocket, went in search of a station official, and grabbed one, who was shepherding people out through an archway.

'Sir! My raven is in one of those left-luggage lockers!'

The official gaped at him, then caught the arm of another, whose uniform was covered in gold braid, because he was the stationmaster. They both stared at Mr Jones, who repeated, 'You can't leave a poor dumb helpless bird in one of those lockers that's liable to blow up. Think what the RSPCA would say!'

Mind you, Mr Jones thought to himself, dumb and helpless was not really a very accurate way to describe Mortimer, and if the lockers *were* going to blow up, which he for one did not believe, the chances were fifty to one that it was because of something that Mortimer had done.

'You can have three minutes to get the bird out,' said the stationmaster. 'No more. Go with the gentleman, Turpin.'

'What's the number on your key?' said Turpin.

Mr Jones looked at the key Dick had given him. But the number on the red plastic disc was blurred. It could have been anything from 0000 to 8888.

There were fifty lockers in each row, four rows deep.

Mr Jones began desperately trying the key in each door that did not already have a key in it. After what seemed about five seconds, Turpin said, 'Sorry, sir. Three minutes is up.' And he firmly dragged Mr Jones out through an archway into Motherwell Road.

Only just in time. Behind them they heard a sudden loud whoosh – like somebody slamming the lid of a huge box made of thick blotting paper. And then the whole side of the station buckled outwards, with tongues of fire coming through between the yellow bricks.

'Lord – a'mighty!' gasped Mr Jones. 'It really *was* a bomb!'

He raced round to the main entrance, where he found Arabel and Mrs Jones clinging together with ashy-white faces, while Annie and Dick Line stood beside them, looking, Mr Jones thought, oddly pleased with themselves, as if they had done something clever.

'Eup. Giggle-giggle. It was us!' said Dick.

'It was those fireworks,' giggled Annie. 'We put them in the locker.'

'I told Annie Dad had got us a box already,' said Dick.

'It was to pay Mortimer back for burning my Winky Doll.'

'Do you mean to say,' demanded Mr Jones hoarsely, 'that it was *you two* who blew up those luggage lockers?'

They nodded several times; little Annie's curried-bean eyes were bright with spite.

'Dick lit the fuses of some of the fireworks, and we put them in the same locker with Mortimer's basket. That'll teach stinky Mortimer to burn up my Winky Doll!'

'Well – if you two did that,' said Mr Jones, 'I don't want to have anything more to do with you. Get yourselves home – I don't care how. Come, Martha, Arabel. I can hear the announcer saying something about a London train. We better –' his voice shook – 'we better get it.'

Annie and Dick walked away, trying to look jaunty. Arabel could hear Dick saying, 'Mean old brute. Anyway I've got enough for the bus home.'

The Jones family had a dreadful journey. The InterCity train sped along towards London at nearly one hundred and fifty kilometres per hour, but nobody had anything to say. Mrs Jones thought of her fur coat. Arabel thought of Mortimer. Mr Jones thought of his house occupied by a gang of reckless smugglers at bay, and surrounded by half the police of North London. What would be left of Number Six,

Rainwater Crescent when they arrived in Rumbury Town? Would it be like the wall of Benwick Station, just a pile of rubble?

When they reached King's Cross, Mr Jones said, 'Maybe we'd best go to Rumbury Central Police Station first. They mightn't want us in the way up at Rainwater Crescent if there's a siege going on, if they've got the street blocked off.'

Mrs Jones said faintly, 'All right Ben, whatever you think.'

Arabel said nothing at all.

The cab driver who took them to Rumbury Central was one of Ben's friends.

'Heard you had a bit of trouble up your way?' he said, and he wouldn't take any money from Mr Jones. 'What's a ride between pals?' he said. 'You'll do as much for me one of these days.'

At Rumbury Central Police Station all seemed quiet and orderly. Mr Jones spoke to the Duty Officer, who said, 'Number Six, Rainwater? The Rumbury Rakes? Superintendent Jarvis would like to speak to you, Mr Jones. I'll see if he's free.'

Superintendent Jarvis was bald and pink-faced, but very different from Auntie Clotilda's pinkness. His was the pink that comes from lots of fresh air, and he had a moustache like two white

waterfalls, and bright grey eyes. He looked at the Jones family in a friendly way, and said, 'How come you heard about the business so quick, if you were up at Benwick-on-Tavey?'

Mr Jones explained about the gold Mortimer bar, and ringing up Fun-Folks Foods Ltd.

'So you just missed being first, eh? That was bad luck.'

Mr Jones felt that the bad luck of losing the first prize was a trifle compared to the loss of the fur coat, the house in Rainwater Crescent, and Mortimer the raven. But Superintendent Jarvis went on, 'I think I can tell you there will be a reward, though – for the part played by your, er, family in helping to effect the recapture of the group of smugglers known as the Rumbury Rakes –'

'Capture?' said Mr Jones.

'Family?' squeaked Mrs Jones.

'Eleven of them.' Superintendent Jarvis counted on his fingers. 'Fork O'Farrell. Lee Lombroso. Guffy Quilp. Duke Scodge. Sam Screen. The Tuna. Nosh Mouch. Milly Mantis. Garfield Coral. Pilligreen Lodge. And Open Winkins. All under hatches, thanks to your, er, family.'

'Family?' said Mrs Jones again.

'Raven,' said Superintendent Jarvis. 'I understand you own a raven?'

Mr Jones cleared his throat. 'Did,' he said. '*Had* a raven.'

The superintendent shook his bald head. 'Nothing *had* about that bird,' he said. 'Wish we had a few like him in my force. Tackled the lot of them single-handed. With –' he studied a typed page in front of him – 'with a do-it-yourself X-ray kit. Your property, Mr Jones? Not sure if they are strictly legal, without a licence, but we'll forget that in the circumstances –'

'I – I'm taking care of it for a relation,' Mr Jones managed to croak out. 'But – but I don't quite understand. You say the bird –'

'The raven, yes. What happened was that the gang, having, at eight-thirty this morning, seen, as they thought, your family depart for what looked like a prolonged absence, at nine o'clock entered and took illegal occupance of Number Six, Rainwater Crescent. They needed an undisturbed spot where they could cut a gold bar into eleven pieces.'

'Wonder why they didn't just sell it and divide the cash?' muttered Mr Jones. 'They had come by it legal.'

'I understand not one of them could trust any of the others to handle such a sale. And they had other things which had not been acquired legally.'

'Awkward job,' said Mr Jones. 'To cut a gold Mortimer bar into eleven bits.'

'Quite. At eleven-fifteen the leader of the gang, Fork O'Farrell, phoned us in some agitation.'

'He phoned the police?'

'Asking for help. The raven, it appears, had descended from a miniature infra-red oven. One of the gang had light-heartedly switched on the appliance, the bird was inside and this annoyed him.'

'It would, yes,' said Mr Jones, nodding.

Arabel, who had sat perfectly quiet all this time, suddenly turned bright pink and said,

'Where is Mortimer now, please?'

'Why, he's at home, at Number Six, Rainwater Crescent, that is, my – Miss; we did suggest he should come up to the station to make a statement, but he, er, declined to do so. You'll find him there – er, PC Halliwell is there too, keeping an eye on the house till you return. I'm sure he will be very happy to see you.'

'Then let's go,' said Mr Jones, standing up.

Arabel turned round at the door to say, 'Excuse me?'

'Yes, my dear?'

'What happened to the gold Mortimer bar?'

'Well that's a bit of a mystery,' said the superintendent, suddenly looking a little forlorn. 'We brought in all the gang without any trouble at all – he had them taking shelter in the larder, the bird did, all –'

'Oh! My Fruity Crumble Cake!' faintly from Mrs Jones.

'– All bar the one who phoned; he jumped out of the landing window and was found on the path outside with a broken fibula. But although we went through that house from attic to garden shed with a fine-tooth comb, not a trace of the gold bar did we discover.'

'Oh well,' said Mr Jones. 'We know the house better than you do. Maybe we'll come across it; if we do we'll let you know.'

'Thank you, Mr Jones.'

The family rode back to Rainwater Crescent in a police car, to the admiration of all the neighbours, who came running out to greet them.

On the ride, Mr Jones said, 'I reckon Mortimer must have wanted to stay at home.'

'He wanted to look at Annie's toys,' said Arabel.

By the time they stopped in front of Number Six, there was a crowd to welcome them, and a hail of cheers. Mrs Jones blushed, and bowed to left and right, like the queen.

Mr Jones, a bit embarrassed, quickly pulled out his latch key and opened the front door. In the hall they found PC Halliwell, sitting, red-faced and stiff, on an upright chair. His right ear was bleeding, quite badly, and he had several tears in his uniform; a button was missing from it.

'Oh dear!' cried Mrs Jones. 'That *is* a nasty ear! You'd better let me put some Cream-of-Wheat-germ Oil on that before you go back to the station. And I'll sew on your button, dear, if you have it.'

'Oh – that's very nice of you, Ma'am, but I'm not sure where it is,' said PC Halliwell. 'And I'd best be getting back to the station, thank you.'

And he left, very fast, on his motorbike, which had been chained to the fence outside.

Arabel looked up to the top of the stairs, and saw Mortimer sitting on the banister rail, looking down.

'Oh, Mortimer,' she said. And she sat down, suddenly, on the bottom stair, as if her legs refused to hold her up any longer.

Mr and Mrs Jones went into the kitchen to make a cup of tea and find out what the Rumbury Rakes had taken, or broken.

Mortimer began coming down the stairs, rather slowly and heavily, thump, thump, thump, thump, until he was on the same step as Arabel; then he leaned against her and she put an arm round him. His eyes were very bright, and he looked exceedingly pleased with himself; as if he had been having a better time in the last twelve hours than ever in the whole of his life before that day.

'Oh, Mortimer,' said Arabel again. 'Were you in the attic?'

'Kaaark,' said Mortimer.

She lifted him and put him on her lap, but he was too heavy to keep there long; he seemed to weigh a good deal more than he had when she put him in his travel basket.

'You won't burn any more Winky Dolls, will you, Mortimer?' said Arabel. 'Ever again?'

'Nevermore,' said Mortimer peacefully.

They never did find the gold Mortimer bar; but the reward for apprehension of the Rumbury Rakes paid for a new hose, and a new doll for Annie, and a new fur coat for Mrs Jones. When Cousin Ray's collarbone was mended, he came and fetched the computer golf, and told them that Cousin Gladys's new teeth had settled in fine.

In Sheep's Clothing

from *More Stories of Clever Polly
and the Stupid Wolf*
by Catherine Storr

*The big, bad but very silly wolf is as determined as
ever to gobble up Polly for his tea . . .*

T HE WOLF stood in the school playground,
waiting for the children to come out at the
end of the afternoon. The parents, mostly mothers,
who were waiting there too, looked at him
suspiciously and none of them came over to speak
to him. He was so very dark, so very hairy. None
of them could remember noticing him there before.

Boys and girls began straggling out of the
building. Some clutched large sheets of paper on
which they had painted portraits of their families.
Others carried egg-boxes, cardboard cylinders

from used toilet rolls, empty cotton reels, shells, nuts, melon seeds and corks, from which they had made pretty and possibly useful gifts. For Christmas was coming, and the children in this school were encouraged to be generous with their time and ingenuity.

The wolf had to wait for what seemed a long time before he saw Polly in a group of children, talking excitedly. This lot carried something different. One child had a pair of large wings in her hand, two more had long, striped robes over their arms, and Polly was carrying a baby doll wrapped in a long white shawl.

'Hi, Wolf!' Polly called out when she saw him.

'Hi, Polly! What's that doll for? I thought you didn't play with dolls.'

'I don't. Not much. Anyway this doll isn't mine, she's Lucy's. I just borrowed her for the nativity play.'

'What sort of play?' the wolf asked.

'A nativity play.'

'What's that?'

'It's about the first Christmas. You know. Jesus being born in a stable and all that. We're acting it the day after tomorrow, and I'm going to be Mary. She's Jesus' mother. It's the best part.'

'A play! Couldn't I be in it too?' he said. Surely acting in a play with Polly and several other deliciously small children would give him a chance to get one of them.

'It's only for my class to act in. And there aren't any more parts to go round.'

'Who else is there besides Mary and that doll?'

'There's Joseph. Benjie is being Joseph. And there're some angels. Sophie over there is an angel. You can see her wings.'

'Why isn't she wearing them on her back if she's an angel?'

'She will when we act our play. There's an innkeeper, that's Michael. He has to say, "No room, no room." And then we go into the stable and I have the baby.'

'Anyone else?' the wolf asked.

'Three kings . . .'

'Couldn't I be a king? I'd be very good as a king,' the wolf suggested, rather fancying himself in a crown.

'No, you couldn't. Derek's one of them and the twins are being the other two. And Marmaduke's being King Herod, who's horrible and wants to kill all the babies.'

'To eat?' the wolf asked.

'I don't think so. And there are a lot of shepherds. They don't have much to say, so they're the children in my class who can't remember long speeches.'

The wolf had brightened at the sound of shepherds. 'Shepherds? With sheep?'

'I suppose so. But no one wants to act a sheep.'

'I would,' the wolf said.

'You? Be a sheep? But you're nothing like a sheep.'

'I could act like a sheep.'

Polly wasn't sure that he could. 'How?' she asked.

'Baaa. Baaa . . . aa. Baa . . . a . . . baa . . . a. Baa!' the wolf said loudly. Several of the parents standing in the playground turned round to look and one or two of them laughed.

'How was that?' the wolf said, pleased with the effect.

'It wasn't bad. But you don't look like a sheep.'

'I haven't dressed for the part yet. After all, when I came out this afternoon, I had no idea I might be asked to be in a play.'

'No one has asked you,' Polly said.

'So when is the performance, Polly?' the wolf went on, taking no notice of this remark.

'The day after tomorrow. Wolf . . .!' Polly began, but before she could finish the sentence, the wolf had gone.

'Benjie. Sophie. Marmaduke. Not to mention Polly. And a lot of shepherds who are too stupid to say anything. I ought to get one of them,' he thought as he trotted home.

When he got there, he went straight to his larder; this was something he always did, sometimes hoping that though he had left it nearly empty when he went out, it might miraculously have filled up in his absence. But the shelves were as bare as before. The wolf sighed, shut the larder door and walked into his sitting room where, on the floor, lay a not very clean, whitish-grey fur rug. It had belonged to the wolf's grandfather, and how he had got it is probably better not to know. It was, in fact, a whole sheepskin, and it was the thought of this priceless possession that had made the wolf so confident that he could take part in Polly's nativity play.

For the rest of that day and for most of the next, the wolf practised. He practised with pieces of string and with safety pins and elastic bands. He even tried to sew with a needle and thread. For most of the time, he practised in front of his long mirror, and at last, on the very morning of the performance, he was satisfied. He not only sounded like a sheep, he now looked like one. After a light midday meal, he carefully dressed himself in his disguise and made his way to Polly's school, using side streets so as to avoid notice.

He managed to slink in at a back door. He heard a gabble of excited voices coming from a classroom further along the passage and, looking cautiously through a glass door, he saw a great many children dressed for the play. He saw a couple of angels in long white nightgowns and gauzy wings. He saw two kings, exactly like each other, wearing golden crowns. He saw several boys and girls in striped robes, with pieces of material wound round their heads. One of them carried a small stuffed lamb under his arm. So these were the shepherds, the wolf guessed. On the further side of the classroom, he saw Polly in a blue dress, with a blue veil on her head, holding the doll baby by one leg, upside down.

The wolf pushed the door open and joined the actors.

'Hey! Who're you pushing?' angrily asked a small stout king in a red robe edged with gold tinsel.

The wolf swallowed a snarl and the temptation to take a mouthful out of a plump leg very near to him, and said, 'I just want to get over to the shepherds.' He knew he would have to be careful until everyone was off their guard and thinking about nothing but the play. He did not want to make a disturbance, and he was particularly anxious that Polly should not see him yet.

'Timmy! here's one of your sheep!' the red king shouted.

'We haven't got any sheep,' a shepherd called back.

'There's one here. Don't know who. Miss Wright must've got someone in extra.'

Lucky, thought the wolf, that no one seemed surprised at this, and no one took any particular interest in him. He lay down under one of the tables pushed against the wall and amused himself by remarking which children were fatter or slower (or both) and so would be the easiest prey. After a short time he noticed that the teacher was looking over each child's costume, hitching up the wings on one angel, tying up Joseph's shoelaces (they came undone again a moment later) and taking the doll baby away from Polly-Mary. 'You don't have the baby in the first scene, that's when the angel comes to tell you you're going to have it,' she said, and put it on a chair.

'Now, we're all going into the hall. Very, very quiet, please. Sophie and Polly, are you ready for Scene One? The others can stand at the side and watch, but no talking and no fighting. Understand?' She gave the three kings a special glare, and led the way out of the classroom.

The wolf trotted quietly behind the children. Along one long passage, turn a corner, another passage, and then a swing door into the hall. People were singing. The wolf caught one or two words: '. . . midwinter . . . snow . . . snow . . . long ago.' It sounded cold and disagreeable. Why not sing about something pleasant, like hot soup, a roast joint? Chips? He found himself jostled among the children and crowded into a small space at the side of the stage, with one of the kings leaning against his shoulder and a shepherd treading on a hind paw.

'I wish . . .' So many juicy little arms and legs all round him. 'But I must wait. If I gave myself away now, I'd never get out of here alive,' he thought, and licked his chops silently.

The singing had stopped. The curtain was drawn back from the front of the stage, and the wolf heard, 'Hi, Mary. You're going to have a baby and it's called Jesus.'

'But I'm not even married!' Polly's voice answered.

'That doesn't matter, because it's God's baby,' the angel said, and walked off. Then Joseph walked on and told Mary they had got to go on a long journey. 'But I'm going to have a baby!' Mary said, and Joseph said, never mind that, she could have the baby in a hotel somewhere on the way.

'When do we get to the shepherds?' the wolf asked a child next to him in a loud whisper. He was bored with all this talk about the baby.

'Not till after the baby's got born, silly,' the child whispered back.

'No talking!' Miss Wright's voice hissed behind them, and the wolf had to wait while Mary and Joseph were told that there was no room in the inn. 'But you can use the stable, if you like,' the innkeeper said kindly.

There was some more singing. The wolf was by now not only squashed, but also terribly hot. The children round him were all warm and excited and he was wearing an extra skin. An elastic band round one of his ankles was too tight, and a shepherd behind him was apt to tread on the

fleshy part of his tail. It was a relief when Miss
Thompson whispered, 'Go on, Timmy, it's the
shepherds now,' and the group round the wolf
moved out on to the stage.

The lights were bright here, and for a minute
the wolf's eyes were dazzled. Then he saw Polly,
in her blue veil, sitting on a stool, surrounded by
bales of straw, with the doll baby on her lap.
Joseph stood behind her. The shepherds moved
towards her and the wolf followed them.

'Hullo, Mary. We heard about your baby, so
we've come to have a look at him,' the largest
shepherd said.

'You're welcome,' Polly said. She still hadn't
seen the wolf.

'We've brought him some presents. Here's an
apple,' one of the younger shepherds said, holding
out the apple.

'Thank you. I'm sure he likes apples,' Polly said.

'And I've brought a lamb,' another shepherd said.

The wolf thought this was a good moment to
give a loud *Baa . . . a . . . a*. Everyone jumped, and
the child carrying the stuffed toy lamb said, 'You
aren't supposed to say that.'

'Why not? I'm a sheep, aren't I? "Baa" is sheep
language,' the wolf said.

'You didn't say that when we rehearsed yesterday,' the first shepherd said.

'I wasn't here yesterday. But I am today. Baa . . . aa,' the wolf said, annoyed.

'He's made me forget what I was supposed to say,' the smallest shepherd said, and burst into tears.

'It doesn't matter, just go on. Thank you for the lamb, it will be nice for Jesus to play with when he's older,' Polly said, quickly.

'You're not the lamb I'm giving Jesus, this is,' said Timmy, showing the toy lamb.

'I don't think he's a lamb at all. He's got black paws,' another shepherd said.

'Some sheep do have black feet. And black noses,' the wolf said.

'He's got a long black tail that sticks out behind, too,' the second shepherd said.

'I haven't! Have I?' The wolf tried to look over his shoulder. There was a tearing sound and the wolf was aware that the fleece was slipping badly and a large safety pin at the back of his neck had come open.

'I don't think he's a sheep either,' Joseph said, interested, and coming round to look.

'I'm not! I'm a wo–' the wolf began, but Polly interrupted. 'Of course he's a sheep. He came in with the shepherds, didn't he? And he's wearing a sheep's coat.'

'Polly, you know who I am. Tell them,' the wolf complained.

'Children, get on with the play, it's time you made room for the kings,' Miss Wright hissed from the side of the stage.

'I expect you want to get back to watch your flocks by night,' Polly said politely to the shepherds, who began to shuffle towards the way out. To the wolf she whispered, 'You stay here. And don't forget, you chose to be a sheep in this play, now you've got to act like one.'

'You mean I've got to go on saying "Baa"?'

'That's right. Just "Baa" and nothing else.'

'Don't I get anything to eat?'

'Sheep eat grass. I don't think there is any grass round here. There's a little straw if you'd like that.'

'Don't sheep eat meat ever? Not a mouthful of leg?' the wolf asked, gazing at the fat little leg of one of the three kings who were now preparing to offer their gifts to the baby Jesus.

'Certainly not! Thank you very much, that'll make a nice smell in this stable,' Polly said to the third king, who had just given her a box supposed to contain myrrh.

'But I'm not an ordinary sheep. And I'm hungry!' the wolf said, rather too loud. The fat-legged king turned round and said, 'Shh! It's my turn to talk now. We're going home without seeing Harold again because we know he means to try to kill your baby. That's all. Bye-bye.'

'Who's Harold?' the wolf asked, wondering whether this was someone who shared his taste in food.

'Herod, not Harold. Don't talk, Wolf. You're not supposed to say anything but "Baa".'

'But that's silly.'

'Sheep are silly. If you wanted to do something clever, Wolf, you ought to have acted a different part.'

'So I've got to go on being a silly sheep and I can't catch anyone? Not even you?'

'I'm afraid so. I'm sorry, Wolf. Joseph and I have got to go now. But you can stay for a bit and go on being a sheep, if you want to. Until we've all gone home, then you can go back to being a stup– to being a wolf again. Come on Joseph, it's time we went to Egypt,' said Clever Polly, and left.

Little Badman / Big Trouble

from *Little Badman and the Invasion
of the Killer Aunties*
by Humza Arshad and Henry White

Illustrated by Aleksie Bitskoff

*Humza Khan, otherwise-known-as rapper Little
Badman, finds the path to fame much harder
than he first thought . . . !*

'"DETENTION"?' SHOUTED my dad. 'What do you mean, "detention"?'

For a second I wasn't sure if he was actually asking me what the word 'detention' meant, or whether he was just angry that I'd got in trouble again. Seriously, it could have been either. For someone who's lived here for twenty years, he's got a weird vocabulary. I swear, he still calls every type of underpants 'knickers' – even his big baggy brown Y-fronts. *Where are my knickers, woman? It just ain't right.*

'It wasn't my fault!' I replied, holding my palms up like it was a robbery. 'They made me stay after school because I saved a teacher's life.'

'Is that *really* all?' asked my mother, who stood beside him in the hallway, peering right into my soul.

'Well . . . I might also have been partly responsible for nearly killing her. But I swear that was mostly Umer's fault. Him and Mustafa.'

'Who is this Mustafa?' shouted my father. 'You are forbidden to spend time with him!'

'Uh . . . OK,' I said. 'I mean, it'll be a great sacrifice. But, if that's the full extent of my punishment, then I agree. You're a harsh but fair judge.'

'Ha!' laughed my dad. 'You think this is your punishment? Ha ha ha! Did you hear that, Nausheen? He thinks this is all the punishment I can come up with for him. Oh, no! No, no, no, no, no!'

I could tell he was starting to go off on one. That was the last thing I wanted. When my dad takes something as a personal challenge, it can only go badly wrong.

'You need discipline, boy!' he continued. 'When I was your age, I ran seventy miles to school every morning and seventy miles back. Sometimes, I was the only one who made it in, including the teachers! I had to teach myself. And did I complain? Of course not! It is what made me the man I am today!'

Ah, man, I'd heard this one so many times I could have mouthed along with him, but I figured that would have only made things worse. So I stayed quiet. Instead I tried to guess which line he'd go for next: *How many shops do I own?* or *Look at the calluses on these hands!*

'How many shops do I own?' he asked.

'Twooo,' I said in that drawn-out way a class says good morning.

'Two. That's right! And how many bathrooms do we have in this house?'

'Threeee,' I replied.

'Three!' he barked back at me. 'Plus one in each shop – that's five bathrooms! No one in my family has ever had five bathrooms. And do you know how I have done so well?'

'Scratch cards?' I began, but he shouted over me:

'Discipline! Without discipline, you will end up like Grandpa!'

Now, just to be clear here, Grandpa ain't my grandpa – he's my uncle. Confusing, right? In fact, he ain't anyone's grandpa – he doesn't even have kids. It's just his nickname because he's so old and tired-looking. Always has been, even when he was at school. At fifteen, he looked like a twice-divorced accountant about to get the sack. By thirty, he was bald and grey and slept twenty-seven hours a day. Nowadays I've got no idea how old he is, but if someone told me he was a thousand I'd believe them.

He looks like he's made of the stuff you empty out of a vacuum cleaner. I think maybe his only purpose in life is to be used in stories to scare little kids into having more discipline. If it wasn't for Auntie Uzma, I reckon he'd have wasted away already.

Now, my mum had remained pretty quiet through all of this. But that doesn't mean she's any less dangerous. They just work differently. My dad's a volcano, blowing his top at the first sign of trouble. My mum, on the other hand, is a carbon monoxide leak. Silent but deadly. She'll get you and you'll barely know she was in the room.

'What do you want, Humza?' she said, when my dad had paused for breath.

'Uh, you mean like for dinner?' I asked.

'No,' she replied. 'What do you want from your life?'

Huh . . . That was unexpected.

See, that's what I'm talking about. Mums work on a whole other level to dads. While my dad's caught up trying to think of a way to throw me out of a window without getting arrested, my mum is getting straight to the important stuff.

'Well, funny you should mention it, but I want – no! – I *need* a Matsani S3000 Home Pro Compact

Video Camera, so I can make the greatest rap video the world has ever seen and –'

'Video camera? What the hell are we talking about?' interrupted my father.

My mum silenced him with a stare.

'And are they expensive, these video cameras?'

'No, man! That's the best bit – only £150!' I replied.

'And do you have £150?' she asked.

'Uh, no,' I replied. I could see by the look on my dad's face that he was as confused as I was about where this was going.

'Well then, *I* am going to help you to get that money,' she continued.

'What?' my dad and I shouted at the same time.

'This boy needs discipline, not a reward!' he yelled, and again my mum silenced him with a sharp look.

'That is all I will say about it for now,' she added. 'We will discuss this later.'

I was so confused by what had just happened that I didn't even hear the doorbell ring. I just stood there next to my dad, our mouths hanging open, trying to figure out what on earth my mum was up to.

'*Hiii-eeeee!*' came the squeal as my mum opened the front door. You can always tell an auntie from their squeal. Each one's was unique. This squeal belonged to Auntie Uzma. She and my uncle, Grandpa, lived two roads away with their cat, David Chesterton.

See, their neighbour, a human named David Chesterton, had died one afternoon a few years back and his cat had just wandered next door looking for food. They didn't know the cat's name, so just started calling it 'David Chesterton's cat'. Before long it became known as David

Chesterton (and occasionally just Dave). It liked curling up on Grandpa, as he spent almost exactly as much of the day asleep as David Chesterton. So that was how a cat named after an old dead white guy came to live with a big round Pakistani lady and her thousand year-old husband. Glad you asked, huh?

Anyway, I was snapped out of my daze by a familiar pinching on my cheeks.

'Who is a beautiful fat boy?' said Auntie Uzma, squeezing the skin of my cheeks between her thumb and forefinger and wobbling them.

'Don't body-shame me, Auntie,' I said. 'Anyway, I ain't fat. I'm big boned.'

'Nonsense!' she said, smiling. 'You are too skinny. But we will fatten you up!'

And, with that, she turned to Grandpa, who was standing behind her, halfway through a big yawn, and snatched the bowl he was carrying. It was a massive pile of gulab jamun, my favourite. If you haven't had them you should. They're these sweet little balls of something. I don't know. And no one makes 'em like an auntie. Or maybe a mum if she's in a good mood – but that ain't often.

'Are these for me?' I asked, reaching for the large bowl.

'No!' she snapped, pulling it away. 'They are for your mother. She may give you one if you are good.'

'Oh, Uzma! Thank you,' said my mum. 'You didn't need to do that.'

'Nonsense. You are too skinny also,' replied Auntie Uzma. 'You are all too skinny. And my cooking is wasted on Grandpa here. I've been trying to fatten him up for twenty years and I get nowhere. So I look after you now.'

'Oh, well, it's very kind of you,' said my mum, taking the bowl.

'You will have some now, yes?' asked my auntie.

'Now? Oh . . . well, we're right in the middle of something actually,' replied my mum.

'Punishing the boy for being an idiot!' added my dad, keen to get back to it.

'Nonsense!' said Auntie Uzma, pinching one of the gulab jamun between her finger and thumb and lifting it from the bowl. 'You will have a little taste right now!'

'Really,' said my mum, 'thank you, but we've not had dinner yet and we're –'

'Just a taste!' interrupted my aunt, holding the little brown ball right up to my mum's mouth.

My mum, who was still clutching the bowl, couldn't do anything to stop her. She either had to open her mouth or have the food smushed against her teeth. So she took a bite, nodding happily.

'Mmm,' she said, before adding, 'Delicious!' when she could manage it.

I've said it before and I'll say it again: aunties are weird. You just have to go with it. And, to be fair, my parents weren't shouting at me any more, so I was pretty happy with the outcome.

'Give her another bite, Auntie,' I suggested.

'Here it comes,' said Auntie Uzma, and she pushed the gooey ball into my mum's mouth again, barely waiting for her to swallow the last piece.

My mum stared at me with quiet irritation as she chewed. I knew I was in trouble . . . Might as well enjoy it while I could.

Of course, at that time, I had no idea *how much* trouble I was in. How much trouble we were all in . . .

The next morning in the classroom, there was no sign of Miss Crumble. There was no sign of any teacher. We all sat there waiting for someone to appear, but no one came. I noticed Wendy Wang had chosen to sit further away than usual and was avoiding meeting my eye. She had on her spare glasses, which were bright yellow and too small for her head. I was just thinking that I might get up and say something to her, when the door burst open and an ogre with a moustache looked in.

'Good morning, children,' said the headmaster.

'*Gooooood mornnnning, Missstteerrr Offallll-box,*' replied the class.

'Sorry for the delay,' he continued, entering the room. 'We've been trying to find a substitute teacher for you, but have run into some problems.'

'Where's Miss Crumble?' asked Wendy Wang, looking upset.

'I'm afraid Miss Crumble's allergy to bees has proven to be rather extreme,' replied the head. 'The doctors say she'll be OK, but, due to the extent of the reaction, she's been put into what's called a medically-induced coma until the swelling goes down. It means they're keeping her asleep.'

Upon hearing this, the class all began to chatter at once.

'Quieten down, students, quieten down,' grumbled the headmaster until the noise settled. 'Now it seems, unfortunately, that there are rather a lot of teacher absences in the borough today, and there's a shortage of available substitutes. As such, we've had trouble finding someone to teach your class.'

'Can't you do it, sir?' asked Wendy Wang.

'I'm afraid I have quite enough other responsibilities to be getting on with, Wendy,' said Mr Offalbox, with a smile that made his caterpillar curl up at the edges.

'Thankfully, though,' he continued, 'we've had a volunteer from the community offer to stand in until Miss Crumble is well enough to return to work. Humza, I believe you two already know one another.'

Before I could even turn to the door, I heard the voice. The shriek . . .

'Hiii—eeeeer!'

It couldn't be anyone else. Auntie Uzma. She was wearing a bright orange shalwar kameez that made her look like an enormous satsuma. Bumping the headmaster out of the way with her bottom, she dropped a large cardboard box on Miss Crumble's desk, then turned to face the class.

'Hello, children,' she said, with a beaming smile. 'I am Mrs Khan, but you can call me Auntie Uzma.'

Then she spotted me. I tried to hide behind Umer, but it was too late. She was over in a flash.

'There's my beautiful fat boy!' she said, squeezing my cheeks in her death grip.

'Gah! Get off, Auntie – I mean, miss,' I said, shaking her off.

'Class,' said the headmaster with a grin, 'Mrs Khan is Humza's aunt.'

'It's true,' said Auntie Uzma. Then she added with a giggle, 'I used to change his nappy when he was so little and fat you couldn't even see his winky!'

Oh. My. God.

The whole class burst out laughing. What was she doing to me? Was this my parents' punishment? It couldn't be. This was too cruel! This crazy old lady was going to destroy my reputation. Destroy my whole life!

'Well,' said Mr Offalbox, grinning right at me. 'I think this is going to work out swimmingly.

I shall leave you to it. Just call if they give you any trouble, Mrs Khan.'

'Oh, don't you worry about me,' said Auntie Uzma. 'I know how to handle these little scamps.'

And, with that, she went to open her cardboard box. The headmaster flashed me one last grin before leaving the room. He was still punishing me; I could tell by the glint in his eye. When I turned back, Auntie Uzma was already handing out the contents of her box. Gulab jamun!

She'd made enough for the whole class and was handing them out, one to each kid. Maybe this wasn't so bad after all. Sure, she was going to ruin my life, but at least it would be tasty. When I got mine, I took a big bite straight away. *Aaahhhhhh,* man, it was good. So good. It kind of made up for the whole 'winky' story.

'It sounds like Miss Crumble's pretty ill,' said Umer between mouthfuls. 'I hope she's OK.'

'She'll be fine,' I replied. 'She's in hospital now. No one dies in hospital.'

'I guess,' said Umer, but he didn't sound convinced.

'Listen, don't worry about that. We've got more important things to think about. Like shooting the rest of the video.'

'But I thought you said my phone was worse than malaria.'

'It is, that's why we're getting that video camera.'

'How? Did you get the money?'

'No, but I'm going to. My mum said she'd help me. She just hasn't told me how yet.'

'Hmm, that sounds a bit too good to be true.'

'Nah, man, I'm sure they've just realized that every day they hold me back from being a superstar is another day they have to live in miserable poverty.'

'Yeah . . . or there's gonna be a catch.'

'A catch? What catch? Why'd there be a catch?'

'I dunno,' replied Umer. 'Mums can be tricky like that.'

Ah, man, I hate catches. What kind of catch could it be? Knowing my mum, it would be pretty bad. I was going to have to play this one carefully.

'Well,' I said, 'all I know is that, one way or another, I'm getting that camera.'

'Great,' replied Umer. 'And, after that, all that's left to do is make the track better.'

'What are you talking about, man? The track's amazing!' I snapped.

'Yeah, it's good . . . It's just . . . you know . . . not . . . *very* good.'

'Whatever. It's gonna be great when it's done. We can work on it more in our music lesson this afternoon. Mr Turnbull said he's got something to show us.'

Let me tell you about Mr Turnbull. For a guy who's, like, seventy per cent bald and wears socks with his sandals, Mr T is a sick musician. He can play pretty much every instrument there is, mix tracks on a computer, and write a beat so tight it makes my dad look generous. He ain't like the rest of the teachers. He's a pretty cool guy. That's why he's helping us with the track. When things work out, maybe I'll make him my producer and rescue him from this place. A lot of big stars do charity work. That could be mine.

'Now, children,' said Auntie Uzma, 'what have you been studying this wee-'

But she never finished the sentence, because that was when we heard the crash. Something heavy in a nearby room had fallen over with a *boom*! It was followed immediately by a terrible scream.

At the time I couldn't be a hundred per cent sure, but, if I had to guess, I'd have said it sounded exactly like a librarian being squashed by a bookshelf . . .

The Watch

from *Quick, Let's Get Out of Here*
by Michael Rosen

Illustrated by Quentin Blake

My mum and dad gave me a watch.
Not a posh watch,
good enough to tell the time by, though.
And it went well enough
until one day at a camp
we were playing smugglers and customs
over the sand dunes.

I was a smuggler
and I had to get £20,000
through the customs
for us to win the game.

£20,000 written on a piece of paper.
There were three ways to get past
the customs.
One – by running so fast
the customs couldn't catch you.
Two – by going creepy-crawly so they couldn't see
you.
Three – going through the customs
with it hidden somewhere.

I chose three.
I chose to hide it on me somewhere.
But where?
'I know,' I said,
'I'll stuff it in my watch,'
and I took the back off my watch
folded up the piece of paper
with £20,000 written on it
and clipped the back of my watch on.

So then I went creepy-crawly over the sand dunes.

They saw me
they grabbed me
and they searched me.
They looked in my pockets

they looked in my shoes
they looked in my socks
they looked up my jumper
down my jumper
down my shirt
in my armpits.
They even looked *under* my watch
but they never thought to look
in my watch, did they?

So they let me go –

and when I got to the other end
where the other smugglers were
I said,
'Hooray, I got through.'
I opened up the back of my watch
and there it was –
£20,000.
I took it out – handed it over
and we had won the game.
I snapped the back of my watch on –
looked at the time and –
my watch. It had stopped.
It was broken.
I had broken it.

That evening I told my brother all about it
and I said,
'Don't tell Mum or Dad about it
or I'll get into trouble.
I'll get it mended secretly.'

So there we were, tea-time
and my brother suddenly goes,
'What's the time, Mick?'
and I went all red and flustered
and I go,
'Er er,'
and I look at my watch
and I go,
'Er er about six o'clock.'
'No it's not,' says my dad.
'It's seven o'clock,'
and he sees me going red.
'Is your watch going wrong?'
'Er – no.'
'Let's have a look.'
'No, it's all right.'
'Let me have a look. It's stopped,
it's broken. How did it get broken?'
'I don't know.'
'What do you mean you don't know.'

My brother was laughing all over his big face
without making a sound.
So then I told my dad
all about the smugglers and customs
and hiding the money in my watch.

He was furious.
'We gave you the watch
so you could tell the time
not for you to use as part of a secret agent's
smuggling outfit.
Well, don't expect us to buy you
presents like that again.'

I was *so* angry with my brother
for getting me into trouble.
Inside I was bubbling.
So –
as soon as tea was over
I went down to our backyard
where there was an old cherry tree
and I broke a twig off it.
It was all prickly and flakey
and covered in a kind of grey slimy muck.

So then I took this twig back upstairs

into our bedroom
and I'll tell you what I did with it.
I shoved it into his bed.
And as I shoved it into his bed
I thought
'This'll pay him back.
This'll pay him back.
This'll pay him back.

He's going to get into bed tonight
after I'm asleep
and his feet
are going to get all
prickled up
and covered in grey mucky slimy stuff.'

Well, later that evening
I was doing some homework
and I had some really hard sums to do.
I couldn't do them.
I was stuck
and my brother – he sees me
scribbling out all these numbers
and the page is a mess
so my brother, he says,
'What's up? Do you want a bit of help

with your sums?'
What could I say to that?
At first, I go,
'No no, it's all right.'
But he goes,
'No, come on – I'll lend you a hand.'

So I say, 'OK,'
and he comes over and he helped me.
He's sitting there right next to me,
my enemy,
showing me how to do my sums.
Then he said,
'Now you try,'
and then *I* could do them.

So there I was, friends with him,
grateful,
I'm saying, 'Thanks. Thanks for helping me.'
But in the back of my mind,
I know something:
THE TWIG WAS STILL IN THE BED.

I didn't know what to say.
All I could see was
THE TWIG
sitting in his bed
just where his feet would get it.

Even if I went and got it out

there'd still be a heap of dirty prickly bits
left in his bed,
after he's showed me how to get
all the sums right.

So I go,
'Look – when you go to bed –
tonight
there'll be a twig in your bed.'

So he goes,

'A twig in my bed? A twig in my bed?
How did it get there then?'
So I say,
'I put it there.'
And my mum and dad heard that.
So my dad goes,
'You put a twig in his bed?
Did I hear that right?
You put a twig in his bed, might I ask
Why did you put a twig in his bed?'

And I just couldn't say.
I just sat there like a lemon.
I couldn't say it was to pay him back for
telling on me about the watch
because they wouldn't think there was anything
  wrong
with him doing that.
So I just sat there
and then I said,
'I don't know.'
What a stupid thing to say.
My dad goes,
'You don't know why you put a twig in his bed?
You don't know why?
The boy's going mad.

First thing he does is smash up his watch
and next thing
he's going round stuffing a twig in people's beds.
He's going stark staring mad, I tell you.'

I didn't think I was going mad.
And I don't think my brother did.

I bet *he* knew why I put
a twig in his bed . . .

from **Charlie Changes Into a Chicken**
by Sam Copeland
Illustrated by Sarah Horne

*Charlie McGuffin has an incredible secret – he can
change into animals. Trouble is, he never
knows when it's going to happen . . .*

'SO . . . YOU'RE like Spider-Man?' Flora
said, frowning seriously. They were all sitting
in the playground in a huddle near the wooden
climbing frame.

'No!' answered Charlie, slapping his forehead.
'We've been through this already. I was nothing like
Spider-Man. I was a spider. I turned into a spider.'

'Hmm,' replied Flora, deep in thought. 'And
you're sure you weren't dreaming?'

'Of course I'm sure!' Charlie said, clearly exas-
perated. 'I was nearly eaten by Chairman Meow!'

'And this happened after you got back from hospital? From visiting your brother?'

'Yes! Straight after.'

'Hmm.' Flora rubbed her chin, thinking hard. 'Hmm.'

'What does "hmm" mean?'

'It's a noise people make when they're thinking,' Flora said in a do-you-really-not-know-that voice. 'Have you never heard someone say –'

'Yes, I know what "hmm" *actually means*. I meant, what did you mean when you hmmed. You hmmed twice.'

'Oh! I see. Well,' Flora replied, a knowing look on her face, 'I think I know what caused this.'

'You do?' Mohsen said, wide-eyed. Mohsen was often wide-eyed.

'You do?' said Wogan, normal-eyed.

'You do?' asked Charlie, narrow-eyed.

Basically there was a lot of eye action going on.

'I do. It's obvious.'

'OK then, Miss Smarty-pants, what's going on?' Mohsen said, crossing his arms.

'So, Charlie, you changed into a spider straight after you were at the hospital, correct?'

Charlie nodded. 'Yup.'

'Well ... I think maybe when you went to see your brother you sat on a needle and accidentally injected your bum with some sort of crazy medicine.'

'I sat on a –? I think I would have noticed if I sat on a needle and injected my bum with crazy medicine!'

'Not necessarily,' Mohsen said gravely. 'I once had an injection on my bum and I hardly felt it.'

'Exactly!' Flora thumped her palm.

'That's completely crazy!' Charlie shouted in disbelief.

'No more crazy than turning into a spider,' Flora said quickly.

Wogan and Mohsen nodded solemnly in agreement.

'OK, tell me one thing.' Charlie held up a finger to illustrate his point. 'Just tell me one thing ... WHY WOULD A HOSPITAL HAVE CRAZY MEDICINE THAT TURNS PEOPLE INTO SPIDERS?'

This question was met with silence.

'He has a point,' said Mohsen.

'Maybe ...' said Wogan. 'Maybe it was medicine that was supposed to turn spiders into people and – actually, forget that.'

'Well, I don't know!' Flora held her hands up. 'It was just a suggestion. I think the only thing we can do is keep an eye on you as much as possible, so we can pick you up and keep you safe if it happens again. And we definitely do not want this happening at the school play.'

In a few weeks Charlie was due to take a starring role in the school play as Sad Potato Number 1.

Yes, that's right. Sad Potato Number 1.

Charlie groaned. 'Oh no! I hadn't even thought of that. What happens if I change into a spider in front of the whole school?'

'Don't worry.' Flora patted Charlie's hand reassuringly. 'It probably won't happen again.'

'Yeah. I'm absolutely sure it won't happen again. But we should definitely keep an eye on you,' said Mohsen sensibly. 'You know – just in case. Except we can't do that when you're at home. So you'll have to tell your parents.'

'I can't tell my parents,' cried Charlie. 'I tried telling my mum but she didn't believe me. And, thinking about it, I don't *want* to tell them. They've got enough to worry about. Smooth Move's got his big scan coming up soon and they're pretty worried, I think. If it doesn't go well, he'll have to have *another* operation and then he could be in hospital for ages more.'

Nobody replied for a moment.

'Look,' said Flora. 'If you want to talk about it, we're all here for you.'

Mohsen and Wogan nodded.

'No,' replied Charlie quickly, blinking. 'Thanks. I'll just have to make sure that I shut my bedroom door if it happens again. So Chairman Meow or The Great Catsby* don't get in.'

* The Great Catsby was Charlie's other cat. But he was incredibly lazy and did nothing except eat and sit in a cardboard box on top of the small fridge in the kitchen. The Great Catsby was highly unlikely to leave his box, never mind run upstairs to eat a spider.

All agreed that this was a very sensible course of action.

But, in fact, Charlie needn't have worried about turning into a spider at home again. What he *should* have been worrying about was turning into a pigeon at school.

Because that's exactly what happened a few days later.

All had been quiet for a week or so. Charlie hadn't changed into any animals. School was still school. His parents were still parenting. SmoothMove was *still* in hospital waiting for his scan. Wogan and Mohsen were still slightly scared of Flora.

But on a slow Wednesday afternoon, during a times table test, it happened again.

'Hey, Charlie!'

This was Dylan. Dylan van der Gruyne was the class bully, and he hated Charlie more than anybody else in the school.

'Hey, Charlie!' Dylan whispered again loudly

'What?' Charlie whispered back, knowing what was coming because he was talking to Dylan and Dylan never said anything nice to anybody.

'You smell like a frog's bum!'

Dylan sniggered to himself.

'No, I don't. Anyway, what does a frog's bum smell like? It might smell nice for all you know.'

Even as Charlie was saying that he realized it probably wasn't the smartest comeback.

'Hey, Teddy!' Dylan hissed at the boy next to him. Teddy was Dylan's best friend and he had a large house, and his mum drove a big Range Rover but Teddy wasn't ever allowed to call her Mum – Teddy had to call her by her name, Lou-Lou. 'Charlie thinks frog bums smell nice. Charlie sniffs frog bums!'

Teddy burst out laughing.

'W H A T I S T H E M E A N I N G O F T H I S Y O U A R E D O I N G A T E S T A N D I A S K E D F O R S I L E N C E.'

That was the teacher, Mr Wind. Arthur Wind was really old – forty-something – and he had grey hair and was pretty nice most of the time, apart from:

a) Whenever his football team, Birmingham United, lost.

b) Whenever Ms Fyre, the head teacher, was off sick.

c) Whenever people laughed during a test while he was on his phone sending text messages (possibly text messages to Ms Fyre, but we can't be certain about that).

They were doing a test and Mr Wind was on his phone.

'YOUKNOWIASKEDFORSILENCE BUTICANHEARGIGGLINGWHAT ONEARTHISGOINGON?'

Whenever Mr Wind was angry he spoke very fast and without punctuation. What he actually said was:

'You know I asked for silence, but I can hear giggling. What on earth is going on?'

None of the children said anything in reply.

'The next peep I hear out of anyone will have them sent quick-sharp to Ms Fyre to explain themselves.'

Ms Fyre was tall, well-dressed and huge-haired. When she smiled, which she only ever did just before she was about to explode with fury, her curled lips revealed vast pale gums and intimidating slabs of teeth. They were teeth designed for pulling chunks of meat off thigh bones. Her office was always warm and stuffy, which made sweat prickle down children's backs

as they stood anxiously waiting for her to speak. The oppressive heat was also perfect for the many orchid plants that were dotted around her office. The orchids were Ms Fyre's babies, and she seemed to care an awful lot more for them than she did for the children in her school. The heat and the orchids gave the office something of a jungle feel: steamy, unpleasant and somewhere you'd be lucky to get out of alive.

A moment later, something hit Charlie on the back of the head. Whatever it was, another one came, pranged off his ear and landed on the floor. It was a paper missile.

Another one hit his neck.

Dylan was pinging paper missiles at him using a rubber band as a catapult.

Charlie swung round.

'Cut it out, Dylan!' he whispered.

Dylan grinned at him. A grin that said: 'I'm really not going to cut it out, but thanks for the feedback.'

Charlie turned back to his test again.

A few seconds later, another missile hit.

'Just cut it out!' Charlie whispered, but just that little bit too loudly.

'RIGHT WHO WAS THAT,' shouted Mr Wind.

Quick as a flash came the reply from Dylan:

'It was Charlie, sir. He's trying to distract me.'

'RIGHT CHARLIE MCGUFFIN I WARNED YOU YOU KNOW THE WAY TO MS FYRE'S OFFICE.'

Charlie tried protesting. 'But, sir –'

'Now, McGuffin!' Mr Wind pointed to the door.

Charlie really tried, but he couldn't help the prickling in his eyes turning to tears as he walked to the door.

He risked a glance at Flora, who gave him a sympathetic smile, and that was it – the tears started flowing. As he shut the door behind him he could feel Dylan's smug smile burning into him.

Charlie's head hung low as he trudged down the corridor. Being sent to Ms Fyre meant a letter home to his parents.

They had enough to worry about with his brother, and now he was in deep trouble at school. He could already see the disappointment in their eyes. The thought made his stomach squirm and his heart begin to pound.

And that's when his left eye started twitching.

Charlie didn't think anything of it until the twitch spread to his other eye. Then, with a surge of horror, he realized what was coming. He was changing again.

The feeling burst through his whole body like an electric flower. It exploded inside him. Every part of his body was aflame, but with a fire that was squeezed and crushed through his veins and arteries and back out through every pore of his skin.

With considerable alarm Charlie saw he was growing feathers. *Feathers!* And the floor was coming towards him fast, which meant he was getting smaller. His legs were growing skinny, and attached to the bottom of the skinny legs were red feet.

And with a flap he saw that he had wings. He had *wings*.

A scream suddenly pierced his ears.

Ms Fyre was striding towards him, a look of total disgust on her face.

Charlie flapped in panic, and Ms Fyre gave another squeal of disgust. She had her arms spread, trying to corner him.

A door suddenly opened next to him. It was Maisie Wand from 1F and as soon as she saw Bird-Charlie she ran off down the corridor screaming. The door was swinging closed, but Charlie saw his opportunity and flapped his way through.

It was a bathroom. With another flap Charlie hopped on to the edge of the sink. And there, reflecting back at Charlie from the mirror, was a bird – a plump grey bird with an iridescent purple-and-green neck.

Charlie was a *pigeon*.

The door burst open and Ms Fyre stalked in, edging round Charlie to open the window.

Then she started waving her arms at Charlie, trying to force him out.

Charlie didn't need any more encouragement. With one beat of his wings he was at the window, and with another he was out and into the playground.

He was free! He had escaped!

He was a *pigeon*!

Settling on the tarmac, Charlie bobbed uncertainly forward, unsure of what to do with himself. Before he had time to gather his thoughts a startling flap of wings nearly made him jump out of his feathers.

Another pigeon had landed next to him. It was pacing back and forth around him, head bobbing, neck feathers glinting in the sunshine. It had gnarled toes and one foot was just a stump, like a lump of popcorn. Its eyes, little black holes in burnt orange, were – and Charlie could not mistake this – staring straight at him. The pigeon cooed, deep and low, and to Charlie's utter shock he realized it was *talking* to him. He could *understand* pigeon. And the first words that he heard the other pigeon say were:

''Allo, you beautiful, delightful little pigeon. My name is Jean-Claude. I am a pigeon. And I am in love with you.'

Charlie wasn't sure he heard him right.

'I . . . I beg your pardon?' Charlie replied. He actually cooed, which came as something of a surprise to Charlie.

'I said, my name is Jean-Claude the pigeon. And I am in love with you. You are the most beautiful pigeon I have ever seen. In the last minute.'

Charlie was beginning to wish that he did not understand pigeons.

'But-but . . . ' Charlie stammered, edging away from Jean-Claude.

'Do not "but" me, *mon petit pigeon*,' Jean-Claude cooed, edging closer. 'Ours is a love that pigeons will talk of for many years. It is a story as old as time – ooh, look! What is this I spy?' Jean-Claude eyed the ground beadily. 'It is a delicious and tasty morsel of food!'

Jean-Claude pecked at something, and chewed it for a few moments.

It was a small piece of gravel. 'Ah! Perhaps not so delicious, after all. Not as delicious as you, my beautiful, delectable pigeon. Now fly away with me!'

'But we've only just met!' Charlie cooed in alarm.

'Ah, but what is time? Time is an illusion! It is capricious like the – ooh, look!' Jean-Claude eyed the ground again. 'A delicious and tasty morsel of food!'

Jean-Claude pecked at something.

It was an old piece of chewing gum that stuck to his beak.

'Mmph! Mmhaphs mmoh mpho mmaphy mmapheh mmah!'

A small battle ensued as Jean-Claude attempted to dislodge the gum. Finally he succeeded.

'I said "Ah! Perhaps not so tasty, after all!"' He flapped his foot frantically at the gum that was now stuck to the end of a claw. 'No matter! We have wasted enough time. We must make haste –'

Another flap of wings startled Charlie and Jean-Claude.

It was a second pigeon. This one was grimy-looking, with greasy feathers. And he was looking right at Charlie, with a beady look in his eye and a greedy look on his beak.

'*Bonjour!* My name is Antoine! I am a pigeon. And I am in love with you, my feathery little pigeon.'

'Oh, for goodness' sake!' Charlie exclaimed.

'I am also looking out for any small pieces of food. I am particularly looking for crumbs,' Antoine the pigeon said.

'Back off, Monsieur Antoine! This pigeon is mine!' Jean-Claude flapped angrily. 'We have been in love for minutes! And any crumbs in this particular region are mine too.'

Antoine bustled. '*Monsieur*, you are not the emperor of crumbs! And you are not the emperor of this exquisite pigeon's heart, for it is I,

Antoine the pigeon, pecker of crumbs and –'

At that, a sudden flap of wings announced the arrival of – you guessed it – ANOTHER pigeon.

'Did somebody mention crumbs? I am – *zut alors!*' The new pigeon bobbed towards Charlie. 'But who are you? What a fine example of pigeon you are! We must fly away together, you and I! A love like ours cannot wait! But first we must eat crumbs!'

'Stay away, new pigeon! This beautiful pigeon and all crumbs in this general area are mine!' Jean-Claude flapped excitedly.

''ow dare you?' Antoine cooed, puffing out his chest. 'This is MY pigeon. But I am prepared to discuss sharing the crumbs in this general area.'

As a heated argument began to break out, Charlie took the opportunity to escape. He walked away, head bobbing, edging as slyly as possible away from the bickering pigeons. He had made it a few metres without getting noticed. And then all the pigeons turned as one.

'*Ma chérie!*'

'Do not go! I am just a foolish love-struck pigeon!'

'We must fly away together, you and I, to pigeon paradise!'

The three pigeons strutted menacingly towards Charlie.

Charlie bobbed backwards away from them.

They strutted quicker, circling him now.

Charlie panicked, as Charlie usually did these days, and he flapped his wings.

He lifted into the air. He flapped more, and rose higher, but the other pigeons took flight too.

'Come back! We fly together!' they called in unison.

Charlie beat his wings harder, rising above the school now. The others followed, though, flying round Charlie, trying to force him down. Charlie pushed his way through the circling pigeons, climbing higher still.

'Some crumbs!' cried Antoine suddenly. 'I'm certain I see some crumbs of food in the general area below!'

'We must peck at the delicious crumbs!' chorused the other pigeons in reply.

And with that all three pigeons flew to the ground and began pecking, leaving Charlie flying alone.

He was flying.

Charlie was *flying*.

With a rush of joy and surprise he realized he was soaring way above the school now. He beat his wings harder, the wind whistling through his feathers. Higher and higher Charlie flew, so free, his heart bursting with happiness.

Silence. The rush of traffic was gone, and there was just the sound of the gentle breeze lifting him.

Charlie had never felt so exhilarated in his life.

Below him he felt, rather than saw, a map, a magnetic map, a rippling field gently pulling him one way, then another.

Higher he flew, towards thick white clouds. The air smelled icy and crisp.

Far below him, the town looked tiny. Fields stretched away towards the horizon. The earth curved gently in the distance.

Charlie hung there, softly beating his wings, suspended by the flowing currents in the air, a mile above the ground.

It was therefore perhaps the worst possible time to feel a charge of electricity shoot through him. A charge of electricity that could only mean one thing.

Charlie was changing.

Back into a boy.

A mile above the ground.

This time, Charlie had no time to panic. He knew he had to do something and do it very, very, very quickly.

He folded his wings, pointed his beak towards the ground and started diving, as fast as he could.

Down he plummeted, his eyes streaming.

500 metres to go . . .

He could feel his face changing. His feet changing.

There was the school, screaming towards him.

300 metres . . .

He felt his feathers disappearing.

Close to the ground. Hurtling down. He had to slow himself. Or the crash would be the last thing he ever did.

200 metres to go . . .

He opened his wings, tried slowing himself, and pulled out of the dive.

100 metres . . .

A lurch upwards.

50 metres . . .

He could feel his wings vanishing.

25 metres . . .

Had to land. Had to –

Charlie crashed on to the ground and rolled. And then just lay there, looking up at the sky he had just been flying in. He wasn't quite sure if he was still alive. He seemed to be – he could see the clouds rolling across the sky, and his bum hurt where he'd landed on it, but he was breathing.

He tried sitting up. He was just about OK. He looked around. By some miracle he had landed in the school field, not far from the bike and scooter rack.

'Charles McGuffin, what do you think you are doing out there?!'

A shout came from an open door. And the shout came from Ms Fyre, hands on hips, her wild bonnet of hair getting wilder by the second.

'Come on, boy, get up! What on earth are you doing just sitting there on the ground? Where have you been? Mr Wind sent you to my office AGES ago! You are in very SERIOUS trouble, young man! COME WITH ME NOW.'

Half an hour later, Charlie was walking back into his class, Ms Fyre's furious telling-off ringing in his ears, and a punishment letter in his pocket, which his parents had to sign. The thought of taking home the news of how much trouble he was in – even more since the pigeon incident – was making him feel sick. His mum and dad had enough problems without him adding to them. He'd let them down. He couldn't help it – he could feel the tears coming again. It didn't help that Dylan was staring at him with a look on his face that was a mixture of gloating and disbelief.

Wogan, Mohsen and Flora were looking at him too, clearly wondering what had happened. He'd tell them later. Charlie slumped to his desk, staring at the whiteboard, trying to hide his face as tears begin to trickle down his cheeks for the second time that day.

'No way! It happened again?' Wogan said, chasing after Charlie as Charlie stormed off ahead of him across the playground.

'Yes,' said Charlie glumly.

'While you were on your way to Ms Fyre? You turned into a pigeon?'

'Yes!' said Charlie, frustration creeping into his voice.

'Hmm,' said Flora.

'Oh, don't you start hmming again. I had enough of that last time.'

'Well, one way or another, we need to get to the bottom of it.'

'No, what we really need to do is work out how to stop my parents from murdering me when they see this punishment letter.' Charlie pulled the

letter out of his pocket. 'Listen to what it says: "Disobedience, lying, evasiveness and all manner of general misdemeanours." What am I supposed to do about all that? I'm dead.'

'Good question,' said Wogan, sounding full of action. 'OK, firstly, who is Miss Demeanours? Is she a new teacher? And *General* Miss Demeanours? Why is the army involved? We need to know.'

Mohsen looked at Charlie and rolled his eyes. Charlie smiled for the first time in quite a while.

The four were quiet for a moment, each lost in thought, until Flora broke the silence.

'It's funny that it happened . . .' Flora paused carefully. 'You know, when you were by yourself. Again,' she added. 'It's just, you know, a bit strange.'

Charlie narrowed his eyes. 'What do you mean "funny"? Strange how?'

Mohsen and Wogan held their breath.

'It's just that, well, nobody else has actually *seen* it happen yet,' Flora said slowly and gently.

'I knew it!' Charlie shouted. 'You don't believe me! You think I'm lying!'

'I don't think you're lying!' Flora protested.

'You do! I can't believe, after everything that's happened, one of my best friends thinks I'm making it all up.'

'I don't!'

'Then what *do* you think?'

'Well, have you considered that perhaps you just *think* it's happening? Maybe your brain is tricking you? The mind is a funny thing and I know you *believe* you changed into a spider and a pigeon but maybe it didn't . . . actually . . . happen?'

Silence hit the four of them again.

Charlie looked furious.

Flora looked like she'd just broken the news to her pet hamster, Rollo, who was two years old, that hamsters usually only live for two years.

Mohsen and Wogan looked terrified.

'Well, you two are being very quiet. What do you think? Do you believe me?' Charlie glared at Mohsen and Wogan.

Mohsen and Wogan sort of muttered and shrugged. They looked nervously at the ground.

Charlie rounded on them, his face red.

'Well, that's just great. Fantastic. Not one of my so-called best friends believes me. Well, you can all just be friends without me.'

And with that Charlie stormed off to the other side of the playground.

He sat on an empty bench fuming silently. And as he sat there, watching a football game between some Year Twos, his anger slowly turned into something much, much worse.

Loneliness.

His stomach felt hollow and yet at the same time like it was full of squirming worms. His head was throbbing and his face was hot and his eyes were prickling with tears again. He wanted to get a hug from his mum or play *Pokémon* with Mohsen or football with Flora or wrestle with Wogan or see SmoothMove again or anything, anything to make this awful feeling disappear.

There really is nothing lonelier, Charlie thought glumly to himself, *than sitting by yourself in a packed playground*. He closed his eyes, if only to stop himself from crying for the third time that day.

'I saw you.'

Charlie swung round at the voice, startled.

It was Dylan.

'What do *you* want?' Charlie said, having thought his day couldn't get any worse.

'I saw you,' Dylan said again.

'What do you mean you saw me?' Charlie said, eyes slanting with suspicion.

'You know what I mean,' Dylan replied.

'Er, no, I don't, actually,' Charlie said, getting more frustrated.

'Yes, you *do*.'

'Look. If I did, I wouldn't ask you, would I?'

'If you call me wood-eye again, I'll thump you.'

'What?! I didn't call you wood-eye! I meant "would I?"!'

'You're just saying the same thing. Anyway, the point is: I. Saw. You.'

'SAW ME WHAT?' shouted Charlie.

'Fall from the sky,' said Dylan.

'Oh! You saw *that*!' cried Charlie, relief flooding him. Not only did he finally understand what Dylan was going on about, but he also had proof that he wasn't going insane.

'What else did you think I'd be talking about? Have you done anything else worth talking about?'

'I guess not.'

'Exactly. Well, I was staring out of the window after you got sent to Ms Fyre and I just saw this thing falling out of the sky. It had wings but then it didn't, and it was too big for a bird, and then it hit the floor and sat up and that was when I saw. Saw it was you. I mean, I always knew you were a freak, but not this much of a freak.'

'I can't believe it! Finally someone has seen me change! I felt like I was going crazy.'

'Calm down, freak boy. So can you just change into whatever you want?'

'I wish,' said Charlie. 'I just sort of change into animals at random. I can't control it. It's useless really. Not exactly a superhero, am I?'

'Hmm. Maybe not.' Dylan thought for a moment. 'Did you poo on anybody's head when you were up there?'

'No. I was waiting for you to come out of class but I changed back before I had the chance,' Charlie said, grinning.

Charlie saw a reluctant smile creep on to Dylan's face.

'And now none of my friends believe me.'

Dylan snorted. 'I don't blame them. If I hadn't seen it, I'd think you'd lost the plot.'

'I guess so . . . But it doesn't matter now. You can tell them what you saw.'

'I'm afraid not.' Dylan shook his head with a hint of sadness.

'But . . . but why not?'

'I'm sorry.' Dylan turned as if to walk away. 'I can't.'

'But why not?'

'Because, Charlie, you're missing the obvious. We hate each other.'

'I don't hate you! I mean, we're never going to be best of friends, but . . . hate?' Charlie was starting to get a sinking feeling that Dylan was perhaps the worst person who could have seen him change.

'Oh, come on. Face the truth. You and I are mortal enemies. We always have been. We always will be. And now YOU have some sort of freakish ability. And that means that I have to try to destroy you.'

'Why are you sounding like a villain in a movie?'

'Maybe I have to build a robot suit or swallow some radiation to defeat you,' Dylan said to himself. 'I'll have to start saving for a lair.'

'OK, that's really not helping the whole movie-villain thing. We don't have to be enemies, you know.'

'Oh, but we do,' replied Dylan. 'We *are* enemies, Charlie, and we can never forget that. We are destined to fight. That's just how stories work, and there's nothing either of us can do about it.'

'But we don't *have* to be! We can be *friends*.'

'Come now. Where's the fun in that?' Dylan gave a wolfish grin and then walked off towards the classrooms.

Charlie watched Dylan disappear into the distance and shook his head.

'What a total nutcase.'

It wasn't until the next day that Charlie spoke to Mohsen, Wogan and Flora again. He had spent a miserable evening at home, banished to his room and banned from his PlayStation after delivering his punishment letter to his mum and dad. They had been very, very angry.

'I'm disappointed in you, Charlie McGuffin,' Charlie's dad had said. He'd actually looked disappointed too. Usually his father was good-humoured; even when he was telling him off, Charlie could always see a gleam in his dad's eyes. But since SmoothMove had gone into hospital, the gleam wasn't there so much.

'We both are. *Very* disappointed,' said Charlie's mum. 'But we both still love you very much,' she added, giving Charlie a warm smile and a lump in his throat.

Charlie had sat in his room for the rest of the evening, simmering with misery, anger, loneliness and, worse than all of those – guilt. His brother was due to have his big scan in two weeks' time and Charlie felt desperate for making his parents angry.

So, when Mohsen, Wogan and Flora all came up to him in the playground first thing the next day, his heart pounded with joy. But he couldn't show that.

'Hey,' said Flora.

'Hey,' said Charlie quietly.

'Hey,' said Mohsen and Wogan.

'Hey,' said Charlie back.

'So . . .' said Flora. 'We've been talking and we thought that maybe we should say sorry.'

'Yeah?' said Charlie hopefully. He didn't really care about the apology; he just needed his friends back.

'We should have believed what you said. We should have trusted you. And we're sorry. Sorry.'

'Yeah,' said Mohsen. 'Sorry.'

'Soz,' said Wogan.

Charlie's heart swelled. He felt it might burst out of his chest with happiness.

'You know what? I don't blame you guys. It IS mad. I wouldn't believe me either. I'd think I was bananas too, if I was you. So let's just forget about it, OK? And hey – guess what?'

'What?' they all replied excitedly.

'You won't believe who can actually prove my story is real . . .'

Noble Warrior

from *The Racehorse Who Wouldn't Gallop*
by Clare Balding
Illustrated by Tony Ross

*Charlie Bass is convinced her horse Noble Warrior
has what it takes to be a champion. But can
she prove it?*

CHARLIE WOKE suddenly in the middle of
the night. Boris was sitting up, his head
cocked towards the window. Outside she could
hear strange noises from the pigs, and the
chickens were clucking as if a fox might be on
the prowl. She pulled on her jeans and trainers,
grabbed a jumper and quietly slipped downstairs
with Boris creeping behind her.

'Shh now, no barking,' she said as she silently
opened the front door.

Clang!

Charlie froze at the sound of a bucket being knocked over. What was going on? Had horse rustlers come to steal Noble Warrior? Maybe someone had seen him at the sale yesterday and followed them home. Or perhaps it was thieves hoping to lift a few bits of farm machinery they could sell on? She had read in the local newspaper about a spate of farm thefts.

Creeping forward, Charlie found the bucket and saw vegetable peelings on the ground. Someone had definitely kicked it over. Pausing for a moment to let her eyes adjust to the darkness, Charlie noticed that the door to the shed where the cows' food was stored was hanging open. And she could hear noises inside – strange crunching noises . . .

The wind picked up, whistling through the trees and making the buildings creak. Charlie shivered. She inched forward and peeked through the doorway. Through the gloom, she could just make out a pale, ghost-like shape.

Boris darted forward and growled.

'Boris, no!' hissed Charlie. 'Come back here.'

The pale shape turned and looked straight at Charlie. Then it made a noise. A low, soft whicker. Immediately, she felt the tension drain from her body.

'Oh, Percy, it's you! Naughty pony. How have you got out?'

Charlie walked towards the pale little pony and put her arms round his neck. Percy was perpetually hungry and, having finished off his share of hay and the rest of Noble Warrior's as well, he must have decided to find more food.

With Boris yapping at Percy's heels like a sheepdog, Charlie led him back to the barn, where she found the gate hanging open. Percy had chewed through the string that had kept it in place.

Noble Warrior was standing quietly at the back of the barn, looking confused. Percy was clearly pleased with himself.

'You mustn't break out,' said Charlie as she closed the gate. 'You might get lost in the dark.'

She looked around to see how she could keep the gate shut and decided the best option was to ram a bale of hay against it so that Percy couldn't push it open. *How to Find the Olympian Within* included a chapter on weightlifting and Charlie knew that female weightlifters not much taller than her had raised more than double their own body weight above their heads. From what she had read, it seemed that leg power was as important as arm power. She looked down.

'Come on then, thunder thighs. It's time to put you to the test.'

Charlie squatted down beside the bale of hay and pushed. It slid reluctantly. She pushed again. And again. Slowly, it inched towards the gate and, ten minutes later, it was in position. She sat on the bale and puffed out her cheeks. Then she crept back to the house and went back to bed.

As morning dawned, Boris stretched and licked Charlie's face. Despite her late-night adventure, she was wide awake in seconds.

'Come on, Boris,' she said. 'We've got chores to do.'

Charlie pulled on Larry's old jeans and a rugby shirt, and ran downstairs in her socks. She didn't own any jodhpurs or riding boots, so jeans and wellington boots would have to do.

She paused at the kitchen door. Her mother was speaking in a low, urgent voice.

'If this doesn't work out, Bill, we'll be in real trouble. I've just got the latest bills and it's worse than I thought. If we can't start paying them off soon, we risk losing the farm and our whole way of life. I can work from a town if

I have to, but you and the kids – you'd be miserable anywhere else.'

'I know, love,' replied Mr Bass. 'But I'm sure it won't come to that. I know we made a mistake, but what's done is done. And it might work out for the best. Charlie thinks we've got a champion on our hands and I believe her. Only time will tell.'

Charlie sucked in her breath. She hoped she was right about Noble Warrior.

Pulling on her boots, she made her way to the barn. Percy had his head through the gate and was munching on the bale of hay she had heaved into place last night.

'You are the greediest pony in the world,' she said. 'Honestly, if I don't keep an eye on you, you'll be as big as one of our cows.'

Percy turned his head sideways and slid it back through the gate. He looked at Charlie with his shiny blue eye, which twinkled with mischief. He was naughty and clever, which is a dangerous combination in a person or a pony.

'So, how are we all?' said Mr Bass with a cheery smile as he walked over. 'What's this hay bale doing here?'

Charlie didn't feel the need to tell her dad

everything that had happened in the night so she just stuck to the bare essentials.

'Oh, the string won't keep the gate shut so I put this across for now.'

'You dragged this here on your own?'

Charlie nodded.

'That's my girl,' said Mr Bass. 'I always knew you'd be a strong one. Said it to your mother the day you were born. This one will be a winner, I said.'

He smiled to himself as he looked over Noble Warrior. 'You sure did cost a lot,' he said, 'but boy oh boy, you're a beauty. Mind you, handsome is as handsome does, so we'd better find out what you're made of. The only question now is, who's going to ride you, eh? I'm too heavy. Harry and Larry are too young and too reckless, and Mum has never ridden in her life.'

'I've been thinking about that, Dad,' said Charlie. 'What about Joe?'

'Joe's a farm boy, not a jockey,' said Mr Bass, shaking his head. 'Anyway, I don't think he'll want to, after what happened to his dad.'

'Well, actually, sir, I would like to. If you'll let me.'

Joe was standing behind them in his farm overalls and boots, a bag in his hand. He didn't look much like a jockey, but there was a fierce determination in his eyes.

'Please let me try. I've got all my gear and everything.'

He started unbuttoning his overalls, which were peppered with a week's worth of milk, cowpats and grass stains. Underneath he was wearing a close-fitting top and light brown breeches. From the bag came a pair of shiny brown leather boots and a black crash hat, covered in a red silk cap. He had an old leather saddle with girths and a saddlecloth, as well as a bridle that looked as if it had seen better days.

'It's my dad's old tack. It's not much, but I think it'll do and, if I clean it every day, it'll get soft again. I polished these last night,' he whispered, showing them the boots. 'I always wanted to be a jockey, you see, but then it all went a bit wrong after my dad died. Mum couldn't bear to see the horses on the gallops every morning, so we came down here and then I had to get a job, so I ended up milking cows. Not that I mind milking cows, sir,' he said rapidly. 'It's just . . . You know, back then I felt I could do anything. Be anything.'

'Well, lad,' said Mr Bass kindly, 'I don't see why not. Your dad was a good jockey so maybe talent runs in your family. Let's give it a go and see what happens.'

Joe's face lit up as if he'd been given every Christmas present he had ever wanted. He walked over to Noble Warrior and patted him gently on the neck.

'You and me, boy. It's you and me,' he said as he tacked him up, adjusting the bridle to fit his head and gently doing up the girth round his tummy.

Mr Bass gave Joe a leg-up and he landed softly in the saddle so as not to frighten Noble Warrior or put too much pressure on his back. Then Charlie led Percy out of the barn and Noble Warrior followed meekly behind. They walked through the farm, past the pigs and the chickens and the cows. Jane Eyre mooed as she watched the procession and Princess Anne glanced at them disdainfully, but the others ignored them.

Harry came out of the farmhouse with a piece of toast in one hand to see what was going on.

'Who's that with the fat pony? Thunder Thigh Thelma?'

'Shut up, Harry,' said Charlie.

'Hey, boys, want to come and see a racehorse gallop?' said Mr Bass.

Harry shoved the entire piece of toast into his mouth, leaving a line of jam on his top lip.

'Yeth, pleathe.'

'Let's hop in the jeep. I worked out what was wrong with it the other day. No diesel.' Bill shook his head. 'Expensive mistake that turned out to be. Anyway it's working now and we'll need it to keep up. A racehorse can gallop at over thirty-five miles per hour, you know. Amazing animals.'

Noble Warrior was perfectly happy following Percy. When Charlie started to run and Percy broke into a trot, Noble Warrior trotted behind them, but if Joe tried to take him anywhere on his own he planted himself to the spot. However much Joe talked to him, kicked him gently but firmly, tapped him down the shoulder with his stick, Noble Warrior would not budge.

Joe turned him in a circle and tried again.

'Come on, boy, let's just have a little canter up the hill. We've got to see how fast you are and we've got to get you fit. Come on!'

He kicked and coaxed, urged and begged, but it was no good. Noble Warrior wouldn't move.

Charlie stood holding Percy with a leading rein. She couldn't run fast enough or far enough to lead him for anything more than a short trot.

Mr Bass was starting to look worried. No wonder no one else wanted to bid for what appeared to be such a well-bred horse.

'Looks like you've bought a dud, Dad,' said Larry. 'We'd have been better off with Strictly Come Chicken Dancing and those painted eggs.'

Harry turned on his little sister.

'Great idea, Charlie! Let's buy a racehorse that costs a fortune, but, better than that, let's buy a racehorse who doesn't gallop!'

Charlie's eyes started to fill with tears. She didn't want to be the one who let her parents down. She didn't want to be the reason that they ran out of money and had to sell the farm.

'Did you say he'd go wherever Percy goes?' asked Mrs Bass, who had heard the hubbub and had come out to watch.

'Yes,' replied Charlie in a wobbly voice.

'Well, in that case, we need to find a way to make that work.'

'I know!' Harry shouted. 'Let's put the ugly pony in the jeep and drive in front of Noble Warrior. Then he'll try to keep up.'

'Don't be stupid,' said Larry. 'We can't put a pony in the jeep. Where's he going to sit?'

Although the suggestion was a daft one, it gave Mr Bass an idea.

'How do you fancy riding Percy bareback?' he said to Charlie. 'It'll be easier than riding Ermintrude and I know you're strong enough to stay on. Let's put those legs to the test.'

He threaded a plait of baler twine through one side of Percy's headcollar, passed it over to the other and tied it in place, creating a makeshift pair of reins. Then he lifted his daughter on to Percy's back and put on her head the same riding hat he'd used when she was a toddler goalkeeper. Except now it fitted perfectly.

'That'll have to do for now,' Mr Bass said. 'Just sit tight and grip with your legs, OK?'

Charlie nodded.

'Be careful,' said her mother.

Charlie nodded again, although she wasn't sure that 'being careful' was really possible in this situation. She looked at Joe.

'Any advice?'

'Take a handful of his mane,' he said. 'That'll help you keep your balance. Don't try to do much, stay relaxed and concentrate on keeping yourself right in the middle of his back. Lean back a little bit and just go with the rhythm. It'll be fine.'

Charlie nodded at Joe. He made her feel calm and more confident. She had to be able to do this. She had to.

Her dad patted her on the leg and turned to Joe. 'You keep Noble Warrior down here until Charlie's got halfway up the field. Turn him to face the other way so he doesn't see Percy's gone. Then let him go.'

Taking a deep breath, Charlie urged Percy into motion.

Mr Bass drove the jeep alongside as they cantered up the field. Charlie clung on to Percy's mane for extra balance and squeezed as firmly as she could with her legs.

Harry leaned out of the car and shouted, 'Come on, Thunder Thighs, grip tight!'

Percy put his ears back flat and bared his teeth at him. Charlie slid to one side of his tummy and forced herself back into the middle.

'Shut up, Harry!' she muttered.

'You're doing great!' shouted their dad from the driving seat. 'I'll stop here, but you keep going for as long as you can.'

He looked back to the bottom of the field where Noble Warrior was not standing still or looking calm. He'd realized that Percy had gone without him and now he was spinning in a circle, rearing and bucking, desperate to catch up. Joe was doing an amazing job of staying on his back as he held the reins tight to stop him from tearing after his little friend.

Mr Bass cupped his hands round his mouth and yelled as loud as he could: 'OK, JOE – LET HIM GO!'

Joe relaxed the reins and Noble Warrior took off at such a pace that he was nearly thrown backwards out of the saddle. The horse thundered up the field, eating up the ground. Joe sat as low as he could, making his body streamlined, his chin just above Noble Warrior's mane.

Clinging on to Percy for dear life, Charlie looked over her shoulder as, with every massive stride, Noble Warrior got closer. He flew past the jeep, leaving Mr and Mrs Bass, Harry and Larry all gasping, and, thirty seconds later, he was level with Percy.

As soon as he was, Noble Warrior put the brakes on. He went from thirty-five miles per

hour to nought in two strides and Joe was thrown forward over his neck. The young jockey clung on and pushed himself back into the saddle.

Charlie was amazed. Percy had just cantered as far as his round belly would take him and was puffing with the effort. Noble Warrior was hardly blowing at all.

'How was that?' she asked.

'*Un-be-leev-able!*' said Joe, his face one big grin. 'This horse is an aeroplane!'

The rest of the Basses came chugging up in the jeep.

'Well, well,' said Mr Bass, smiling at his family. 'Looks like we've got a racehorse on our hands. Now all we have to do is make him want to gallop on his own.'

Then Charlie understood why no one else at the sales had been interested in Noble Warrior and why Eamon had been so keen to get rid of him. He might have been bred to be a racehorse, but he didn't want to run: he just wanted to be with Percy.

But, thought Charlie to herself, *if we can work out a way to make one desire help the other then all our problems are over!*

Dragons at Crumbling Castle
by Terry Pratchett

Illustrated by Mark Beech

*Dragons have invaded Crumbling Castle, and all
of King Arthur's knights are either on holiday or
visiting their grannies . . .*

IN THE days of King Arthur there were no
newspapers, only town criers, who went around
shouting the news at the tops of their voices.

King Arthur was sitting up in bed one Sunday,
eating an egg, when the Sunday town crier trooped
in. Actually, there were several of them: a man to
draw the pictures, a jester for the jokes and a
small man in tights and football boots who was
called the Sports Page.

'DRAGONS INVADE CRUMBLING
CASTLE,' shouted the News Crier (this was the

headline), and then he said in a softer voice, '**For full details hear page nine.**'

King Arthur dropped his spoon in amazement. **Dragons!** All the knights were out on quests, except for Sir Lancelot – and he had gone to France for his holidays.

The Ninth Page came panting up, coughed, and said: 'Thousands flee for their lives as family of green dragons burn and rampage around Crumbling Castle . . .'

'What is King Arthur doing about this?' demanded the Editorial Crier pompously. 'What do we pay our taxes for? The people of Camelot demand action . . .'

'Throw them out, and give them fourpence* each,' said the king to the butler. 'Then call out the guard.'

Later that day he went out to the courtyard.

'Now then, men,' he said. 'I want a volunteer . . .' Then he adjusted his spectacles. The only other person in the courtyard was a small boy in a suit of mail much too big for him.

---

* In the days of King Arthur, this was a lot more money than it seems today – it would buy, oh, at least a cup of mead and a hunk of goat's meat.

'Ralph reporting, sire!' the lad said, and saluted.

'Where's everyone else?'

'Tom, John, Ron, Fred, Bill and Jack are off sick,' said Ralph, counting on his fingers. 'Then William, Bert, Joe and Albert are on holiday. James is visiting his granny. Rupert has gone hunting. And Eric . . .'

'Well then,' said the king. 'Ralph, how would you like to visit Crumbling Castle? Nice scenery, excellent food, only a few dragons to kill. Take my spare suit of armour – it's a bit roomy, but quite thick . . .'

So Ralph got on his donkey and trotted over the drawbridge, whistling, and disappeared over the hills. When he was out of sight he took off the armour and hid it behind a hedge, because it squeaked and was too hot, and put on his ordinary clothes.

High on a wooded hill sat a mounted figure in coal-black armour. He watched the young boy pass by, then galloped down after him on his big black horse.

'HALT IN THE NAME OF THE FRIDAY KNIGHT,' he cried in a deep voice, raising his black sword.

Ralph looked round. 'Excuse me, sir,' he said. 'Is this the right road to Crumbling Castle?'

'Well, yes, actually it is,' said the knight, looking rather embarrassed, and then he remembered that he was really a big bad knight, and continued in a hollow voice, '**BUT YOU'LL HAVE TO FIGHT ME FIRST!**'

Ralph looked up in amazement as the black knight got off his horse and charged at him, waving his sword.

'Yield!' the knight yelled, then he got his foot stuck in a rabbit hole and tripped over in a great clatter, like an explosion in a tin factory. Bits of armour flew everywhere.

There was silence for a moment, and then the helmet unscrewed itself and Ralph saw that the Friday knight himself was a very small man indeed. Or, at least, he had a very small head.

'Sorry,' said the knight. 'Can I try again?'

'**Certainly not!**' said Ralph, and unsheathed his rusty sword. 'I've won. You've fallen over first.*

---

* That's how it went in those days: the first knight to fall over lost the fight. I bet you all knew that.

It's not even Friday, so I shall call you Fortnight, 'cos I've fought you tonight. You're my prisoner!'

There was a great deal of clanking inside the armour, and then Fortnight climbed out through a trap door in the back. His ferocious black armour was three times as big as he was.

So Ralph continued his journey to Crumbling Castle on his donkey, followed by Fortnight the Friday knight on his great black charger. After a while they became quite friendly, because Fortnight knew lots of jokes and could sing quite well. He'd belonged to a circus before he became a knight.

Next day they found a wizard sitting on a milestone, reading a book. He had the normal wizard's uniform: long white beard, pointed hat,* a sort of nightdress covered in signs and spells, and long floppy boots, which he had taken off, revealing red socks.

'Excuse me, sir,' said Ralph, because you have to be careful when talking to wizards. 'Is this the way to Crumbling Castle?'

---

* No self-respecting wizard would be seen in public without a pointy hat. But it could make going through low doorways a bit tricky, so they often developed bad knees in later life due to all that crouching down.

'Thunder and lightning! Yes,' said the wizard, closing his book with a snap. 'Do you mind if I come too? I've got a few anti-dragon spells I'd like to try out.'

He said his name was Fossfiddle, and he was sitting by the road because his magic seven-league boots had broken down. He pointed to the pair of high brown boots by the milestone: magic boots are handy things – you can walk as far as you like in them without getting tired – but Fossfiddle's needed a bit of work on them.

So they gathered round, and since Fossfiddle knew a bit about magic and Fortnight knew a bit about boots and Ralph knew a bit about walking, they soon had the boots working again. Fossfiddle put them on and trotted along by Ralph's donkey.

The land around them grew grimmer and grimmer, and black mountains loomed up on either side. Grey clouds covered the sun, and a cold wind sprang up. The three of them plodded on, and came to a cave hidden in a clump of thorn bushes.

'We could do with a fire,' said Ralph.

'Nothing easier,' said Fossfiddle. He muttered something, and produced a funny-looking glass bulb, a small hat,

a banana and a brass candlestick. It wasn't that he was a bad wizard: he just got things mixed up. And if he had but known it, the funny-looking bulb was several centuries ahead of itself.

After Fortnight had lit a fire they settled down around it and Ralph and Fossfiddle dozed off. But Fortnight thought he could hear something.

Crack! went a stick in the bushes. Something was creeping towards them.

Fortnight picked up his sword and crept towards the bushes. Something was moving in them; something with very large feet. It was very dark, and somewhere an owl hooted.

'**YIELD!**' yelled Fortnight, and dashed into the bushes. This woke up Ralph and Fossfiddle, who heard a great cracking and bashing about going on. So up they got and ran to Fortnight's help.

For five minutes there was no sound to be heard but swishings – and swear words when people trod on thorns. It was so dark nobody knew if anything was creeping up behind them, so they kept turning round and round just to make sure.

'**I'VE GOT IT!**' shouted Fortnight, and jumped on something.

'Me!' came Fossfiddle's voice from the leaf-mould.

While all this was going on something very small crawled out of the bushes and began to warm its feet by the fire. Then it rummaged through the rucksacks and ate Fossfiddle's breakfast for tomorrow.

'I heard something, I tell you,' muttered Fortnight, as the three of them came, scratched and bruised, out of the brambles. 'Look, there it is!'

'It's a dragon! shouted Fossfiddle.

'It's a very weeny one . . .' said Ralph.

The dragon was about the size of a small kettle; it was green and had very large feet. It looked up at them, sniffed a bit, and began to cry.

'Perhaps my breakfast didn't agree with it,' muttered Fossfiddle, looking at his rucksack.

'Well, what shall we do with it?' said Ralph. 'It doesn't look very dangerous, I must say.'

'Has it lost its mummy then?' cooed Fortnight, getting down on his hands and knees and smiling at it. It backed away, and breathed some smoke at him. Fortnight wasn't very good with children.

Finally they made it a bed in a big saucepan, put the lid on, and went back to sleep.

*

When they set off next morning Fossfiddle carried the saucepan on his back. After all, they couldn't just leave the dragon behind. After a while the lid opened, and the dragon stared out.

'This isn't dragon country,' said Ralph. 'I suppose it must have got lost.'

'It's the green variety. They grow to be thirty feet tall,' said Fortnight, 'and then they take to roaring and rampaging and walking on the grass and other lawlessness and wicked deeds.'

'What sort of deeds?' asked Ralph interestedly.

'Oh – well, I don't know. Leaving taps running and slamming doors, I suppose.'

That afternoon they came to Crumbling Castle.

It was on a high hill all by itself, and built of grey stone. In the valley below was a town, but most of it was burned down. There was no sign of anybody, not even a dragon.

They plucked up the courage to knock at the big black door. Fortnight's knees were knocking, and since he was wearing armour, this made a terrible din.

'There's no one in,' he said quickly. 'Let's go back!'

The door wouldn't open, so Fossfiddle got out his spell book.

'Hopscotchalorum, Trempledingotram-lines!' he chanted. '*Open!*'

Instead the door turned into pink meringue. Fossfiddle always got things wrong.

'My word, dashed tasty door that,' said Fortnight, when they finally got through. They were in an empty courtyard. It seemed they were being watched. 'I don't like this much,' he added, looking around and drawing his sword. 'I get the feeling that something is going to jump out on us.'

'That's very nice, I must say,' said Fossfiddle, whose nerves were not as good as they had been.

'It's all right,' said Ralph. 'Dragons are seldom bigger than the average house and not much hotter than the average furnace.' He trod on Fossfiddle's cloak as the wizard tried to run away. 'So come back.'

Just then they met a dragon. It looked quite like the one asleep in the saucepan in Fossfiddle's pack, except it was much MUCH bigger.

It crawled across the courtyard to them.

'Morning,' it said.

Now this placed our heroes in a bit of a quandary, as you can see. You can't go off and kill something that's just said good morning to you.

'Good morning,' said Ralph, rather embarrassed. 'I suppose we've come to the right place?'

'Yes, this is Crumbling Castle. I suppose you've come about all these people who've been bothering us.'

'First we've heard,' said Ralph. 'We heard that you dragons were bothering people. Where is everyone, anyway?'

The old dragon yawned. 'Down at the dragon caves.'

Then he explained it all to them. Dragons were really quite peaceful, and these had been living in some caves down by the river, bothering no one except the fish, which they ate. But then the lord of the castle had built a dam downriver, and their caves had been flooded out.

So the dragons had come to live in the castle, scaring everyone else away. They had burned a few houses down, but they always checked that there was no one at home before they did so.

While the old dragon was talking, other dragons came from various parts of the castle and sat around listening.

'And now they've come and kidnapped the dragon prince,' said the dragon.

'Is he about twelve inches long, with large paws and a habit of biting?' said Fossfiddle suspiciously. 'Because if he is, we found him a few days ago. He'd just got lost.' He held out the saucepan, and the little dragon hopped out.

There had to be a lot of explaining. Fortnight went down to the river and found the lord hiding up a tree, and brought him back. Most of the other castle people followed the lord.

'I'm afraid there's no possibility of taking the dam down,' said the lord, hiding behind Fortnight. 'We built it for a swimming pool.'

'You don't have to,' said Ralph. 'All you need to do is build a few caves out of bricks or something.'

So they did. The three fighters pitched in and helped, and it wasn't long before they had a nice row of caves, with hot and cold running water and a bath in each one. The dragons took to them at once, and agreed to leave the castle.

'I suppose that's it then,' said Ralph, as they strolled away from the castle with all the dragons and people waving to them.

'Good job for the dragons there wasn't any fighting,' said Fossfiddle, 'or they might have found out a thing or two!'

They had a good laugh about that, and disappeared over the hill.

The Geek Squad
by Rebecca Elliott

When the Geek Squad come under attack from
bullies, clever TJ seeks revenge with an ingenious,
crazy plan.

HEY THERE, dudes and dudettes!
My name is Tilly Jane Stanley. But you
can call me TJ. I'm ten years old, about as tall as
five cats standing on top of each other (which they
do not like to do, believe me, I've tried), my hair
is more mop than hair and when I grow up I'm
going to be a superhero. Or maybe a mad scientist.
Or maybe a mad superhero scientist.

My favourite things are: parties, the word
BAMBOOZLE, cake mixture (one day I'm going
to make a big bowlful and eat it all BEFORE it gets

made into a cake and RUINED), the colour orange and making things – especially a big fat mess.

I live in Granger Road with my housemates. Otherwise known as The Stanley Family: my mum – she's an artist. She makes sculptures and stuff, and sings loudly, and badly, ALL the time. And my dad – he's really tall. His name is Peter, so everyone calls him 'Two-Metre Peter'. He works in the city – nobody knows what he does, so he may be a spy. Or a Financial Audit Manager. We're not sure.

And then there's my dog, Harvey. He snores, digs holes, eats shoes and scares himself when he farts.

I DID live next to my best friend, Stewie. He once drew a moustache and a monocle on his baby brother. In permanent marker. His mum and dad had to buy his brother a top hat just to complete the look until the ink faded. But last week he moved away, which makes my insides feel super sad.

The new kids that live in Stewie's house look full-on weird. The girl has bare feet, only wears black clothes and has dead flowers in her hair. And her older brother has greased-down hair and carries a briefcase. An actual briefcase. At ALL times.

My neighbours on the other side are no good either. That's where Jacko lives.

Jacko is eleven and super cool. He has cool hair, he hangs out in his great big cool den in his garden with his cool friends, Abi and Kieran. And he hates me. In fact, he hates most people. He thinks it's super cool to bully everyone younger or less cool than him – which kind of makes him not cool.

Jacko's gang are also mean to the teachers at school – even the nice ones! Like the head teacher, Mr Pretty. I know, Mr Pretty is a silly name but he's actually all right and we all kind of like him. His tie is always over one shoulder so even if he's standing still it looks like he's moving fast. And he has a moustache that dances when he talks. But Jacko and his gang do NOT like him. Mostly because he puts them in detention a lot for bullying other kids. Like me. Also, because Mr Pretty lives on our street. And is friends with all of our parents. Which Jacko HATES. Sometimes I hear him shouting at his parents, things like, 'HOW CAN YOU BE FRIENDS WITH A TEACHER?! THEY'RE THE ENEMY!'

I don't mind living near the head teacher. But I DO mind living next door to the school bully. If

I go out in my garden, Jacko and his mates say something really unfunny like, 'Hey look – it's Pee-Jay. Or is that WEE-Jay? Peed yourself lately, PEE-Jay?'

I politely tell them it's actually TJ, but they don't get the message because they have the brains of early man. Then they say something like, 'Want some sweets, Pee-Jay?' before pelting me with half-chewed old toffees. Being rained on by confectionery isn't nearly as sweet as it sounds.

It's the beginning of the two-week Easter holidays. My best friend has moved away. My back garden is not safe to play in. I'm lonely. And bored. And under attack.

Should I just give up and stay in my room?

HECK NO!!

I'm TJ Stanley, I never give up! I make things! I'll make my own happy! Time to make plans, (make myself a sandwich . . . mmm . . . yum), make my first move and MAKE . . . yes, it's happening . . .

BRAIN WAVE!

I'll make a force field around my garden to keep out Jacko and the stuff he throws at me!

Hmm. But now I've looked it up on the internet. It seems even the best scientists in the world haven't been able to make a force field yet.

Think again . . .

BRAINWAVE 2!

This time I've GOT it! I'm going to MAKE . . .

Drum roll please . . .

THE MOST AWESOME DEN YOU HAVE EVER SEEN! IT WILL HAVE TOWERS, SLIDES, DRAWBRIDGES. IT WILL BE TALLER THAN JACKO'S, BIGGER THAN JACKO'S AND ONE HUNDRED TIMES MORE BRILLIANT THAN JACKO COULD HAVE IMAGINED IN HIS COOLEST ELEVEN-YEAR-OLD COOL DREAMS!!!

It will be my fortress of safety against Jacko and his henchmen.

I spend a day getting together a load of stuff to use including:

- blankets
- cardboard
- an old mini fridge from the garage
- big flowerpots I can turn over and use as chairs
- loads of wood I found in the shed that Dad *probably* won't miss

- some huge coloured see-through plastic sheets left over from Mum's recent art installation (Mum's last piece was a spray-painted black saucepan hanging in a multi-coloured plastic cube and it was called, 'Banana'. Hmm, I don't understand it either . . .)

Then I spent two days planning, drawing, waiting for Jacko to go out so I could get in my back garden without being fired at, building and . . .

. . . finally . . . the den is finished!

Then just as I was admiring my awesome handiwork . . . it fell to the ground in a big CRASH! And I realized that maybe, just maybe, I need a *little* bit of help with this. But Mum and Dad are working and my best friend has moved away. So, in desperation, I decided to call on the other weirdo kids on my street.

First up – Charlie.

Charlie is a year younger than me but twice the size. He always has a cheeky grin on his face and a spoon in his pocket, just in case there's eating to do.

I get him round mine and, after scoffing his 'favourite' meal from our fridge (leftover pizza, some chutney and an apricot yoghurt), I tell him about my den plan. Charlie likes the plan because Jacko picks on him too, but mostly because I tell him there'll be a mini fridge in our new den. He raises his hand to offer me a high-five in celebration. Then, instead of my hand, he slaps me in the face shouting, 'Face-five!' and then laughs hysterically. Charlie's sense of humour is a bit strange.

Next up, we decide to recruit Daisy from down the end of the street. On the way there we pass Mr Pretty who gives us a friendly 'hello, you two', his moustache dancing around on every syllable. Then he asks us to give an invite to our parents to join him for 'drinks and nibbles' at his house on the last evening before school starts again.

'Don't worry, you kids don't have to come, I know that wouldn't be very cool!' he laughs.

He's all right, Mr Pretty – a bit of a nerd, but all right – so we agree to pass on the invite.

Then we get to Daisy's house. Daisy has sunshine-coloured hair, always in perfect plaits, she wears dresses, even when she doesn't have to, and her favourite things are ponies, princesses and the colour pink. If there was ever a royal pink pony born, she'd probably wet herself with excitement.

Jacko bullies Daisy too. So she agrees to help with the den, as long as she can decorate it with glitter pens.

Then we all go round to Stewie's old house next door. The door creaks open, like the door to a haunted house in a movie.

We all take a step back.

The creepy girl in black appears then presses the witch's laugh noise on a sound machine as she puts her head back and silently mime-cackles along.

'Hey, I'm TJ,' I say, while Charlie and Daisy shuffle their feet awkwardly behind me. 'I live next door, and these two live down the road. What's your name?'

'February,' she says in a strange high-pitched slow voice that sounds like a drunken mouse.

'Wow, OK,' I say, a bit weirded out – not only because of the sound machine, but because February is NOT normally a name. But then, I think, she was probably born in February, which kind of makes some sense, so I say, 'Oh, I know why your parents called you that – when's your birthday?'

'July,' she says, before adding, 'I have to go and feed my turtle now. Bye bye, TJ.'

I'm not even sure she has a turtle. I tell you, the girl is odd.

'Hang on!' says Charlie, before she can shut the door on us. We tell her about the den. And how it will help us all not get bullied by Jacko. She agrees, but only if we let her brother Gilbert, the one with the briefcase, in. She tells us he's a 'total genius' at maths, engineering, design, all that kind of stuff. He'd know how to build it. I say I'll have to consult my colleagues, so Charlie, Daisy and me walk back to the road and have a whisper-meeting.

'We need Gilbert,' whispers Daisy.

'But, Daisy. He is NOT cool. He carries a briefcase! We cannot have him in our gang,' I say.

'Then you're just a bully like Jacko and I don't want to be in your "gang" any more,' says Daisy, folding her arms. 'Come on, Charlie, we're leaving.'

Charlie shrugs and follows her down the road.

Daisy's right. I don't want to be like Jacko. I don't want to decide who is and isn't cool enough. I want to be the anti-Jacko.

'Wait!' I yell, running after them.

They stop and turn.

'We're listening.'

'OK, I was mean. I'm sorry – let's get Gilbert.'

Daisy smiles and Charlie face-fives me. I say 'Ow', and we go back to February and Gilbert's house and recruit them into our gang of dweebs, misfits and weirdos – otherwise known as The Geek Squad.

The next day, The Geek Squad assembles and we all brainstorm our ideas for the den. Daisy wants a pink princess tower and a tiny fairy door, Gilbert wants a telescope and science lab, February wants an attic with bats living in it and a real skeleton, I want hammocks and a disco floor and Charlie just wants a well-stocked fridge. And a snack trunk.

We took a few ideas from everyone and came up with a final design, which Gilbert drew on his computer all 3D and everything. It turns out he is pretty cool, after all. And a bit of a genius.

Although at one point he screamed as he thought he saw a giant bug coming to attack us, then realized it was a tiny bug on his glasses. Proof that you can be a genius and a complete numpty all at the same time. Who knew?

Over the next week we work together and build the den, with one person on lookout to see when Jacko is out and it's safe to go in the garden (we got it wrong once and Jacko's gang pelted us with half-eaten sweets). Then our luck was in – Jacko went on holiday for a few days (my mum found this out from his mum. Mums find out everything from other mums. Dads know nothing). And then it was finished. We stood back and admired our work.

Our den has a slide, telescope, fridge, snack trunk, sofa (made from big flowerpots), dog bed for Harvey (a cardboard box with my mum's furry red hoodie in it. She'll never notice. Although it already smells of dog farts), a big painting of a skull on the outside, a pink lookout tower (or 'princess tower', if you're looking at it through Daisy's eyes), windows that actually open, hammocks and a fairy door.

I know. Totally, splendidly, awesome!

The outside is made out of Mum's big colourful plastic square panels. It looks a bit like it's made from toy building blocks, so we've called it The Blockhouse. Which only makes it cooler.

Today was our first day hanging out in the den. We didn't see or hear anything from Jacko.

Maybe I was right! Maybe Jacko has seen that our den is bigger, better and stronger than his and he'll leave us alone now! But then . . .

We were playing Spoon Balloon, a little game of my own invention in which you each have a spoon and you have to use it to hit the balloon to each other. I mean the clue's in the title really.

When suddenly, WHACK!

While we all tried to work out what made the sound, Gilbert went outside to see and was hit square in the face with a water balloon, knocking his glasses off and breaking them in two.

'My eyes!! My beautiful eyes!!' he screamed as he ran back inside.

We all ducked and heard Jacko's voice. 'Listen up, little nerds. Just because you've built yourself a fortress doesn't mean we need to stop throwing things at you.'

We could hear his henchmen, Abi and Kieran, giggling in the background.

'In fact, you've given us a bigger target to aim at – thank you!' said Abi.

Then, WHACK! WHAM! SPLAT! SPLOSH!

We were under fire! The water bombs came through the windows and knocked our pink tower off. One hit Daisy in the – well, frankly – in her butt, and one soaked the contents of Charlie's snack trunk. I've never seen the boy so upset.

He fell to his knees, like a soldier on the battlefield over the body of his injured friend, and yelled 'WWHHYYY????!!!' with his hands up in the air.

Eventually, after the firing stopped, we heard Jacko's crew laughing. Then Jacko said, 'Have you had enough yet, little dweebs?'

'Erm . . . yes, no more, thank you, Jacko.' I shouted.

We stayed crouched down for ages, no one daring to move. Then Daisy peered through the telescope and saw that Jacko and his mates had got bored and gone indoors.

'I'll help you clear up, and then I think we should all go home,' said Daisy.

'She's right, TJ, this isn't going to work,' said Gilbert, fixing his glasses with sticky tape from his briefcase.

'It's like Jacko said, we've just given him a bigger target to aim at. We can't hide from him in this massive thing,' said Charlie, with a mouth full of soggy chocolate biscuit.

'Then let's stop hiding!' I said. 'Let's stand up to him. Look, I know he's big, and scary, and . . . cool, but we're . . .'

'We're just a bunch of little geeks,' said Daisy, twiddling her plaits in her fingers sadly.

'Not a bunch. An army. A squad!' I said. 'So, let's be proud of that – we are The Geek Squad. We stand up to bullies, stick up for all the little nerds out there and don't give up after the first battle!'

I think my little speech worked because everyone started to get excited! Even February, who so far had been lying on the floor staring at nothing, jumped up.

'She's right, y'know. There's more of us than them, and we're cleverer.'

'Exactly! Thank you, February.'

'And the spirits of the dead are on our side.'

'Exactly! Wait, what?' I said, before I remembered that February's strangeness is what makes her cool.

We fixed The Blockhouse and then we came up with a plan – find out when Jacko's next attack on us is, and FIGHT BACK.

The next day was the final day of the holidays. We spied on Jacko and his gang and saw something very strange indeed . . .

Through the holes in the fence we could see Jacko, Abi and Kieran over the other side of the garden on their hands and knees in his mum's flower beds, with trowels and buckets!

'What? Jacko's gang are secret . . . gardeners?' said Charlie, laughing.

'No, wait!' said Gilbert taking a closer look from up in the tower, through the telescope. 'They're not gardening – they're collecting worms!'

'It must be for their next attack on us!' said February. 'You've got to admire their inventiveness.'

Daisy's face went green. 'If a worm even TOUCHES me, I will scream louder than you have ever heard anyone scream in your life! I'm going home!'

'No, wait!' I said. 'Look – they're going back to their den now. Let's find out when they're going to worm-attack us and we can protect ourselves.'

Daisy agreed to stick around at least until we found out what they were up to. February, in her ninja costume, crept over the fence to spy on Jacko and his gang. Which was either really brave, or really stupid.

She held Gilbert's walkie-talkie up to their den while we listened in on the other. We expected to hear them planning their next attack on us, probably this evening while our parents were all at Mr Pretty's Drinks and Nibbles evening. But instead we discovered something way worse.

They were planning a worm attack, but not on us ... on our head teacher, Mr Pretty! At his house, tonight!

'We have to protect Mr Pretty!' said Gilbert.

'Why?!' spluttered Charlie, who was now on his third tube of Pringles.

'Because he doesn't deserve a face full of worms in front of the whole street!' said Daisy.

'AND because we're The Geek Squad!' I said, standing up with my hand over my chest, ' "sworn to protect geeks everywhere" – and what are teachers if not overgrown geeks?!'

Everyone stood up as we all shouted, 'Geek Squad Assemble!' together. Apart from Charlie who face-fived all of us.

We knew we couldn't just tell Mr Pretty, as then Jacko would know it was us and would just bully us more. So, we came up with another plan to save Mr Pretty from a wormy fate.

First, we all put on ninja warrior costumes. We used February's black tights, some of my Mum's old black t-shirts she uses to paint in and my Dad's black pants for masks.

Then when the light was fading, about half an hour before the guests were due at Mr Pretty's house, we hid in the bushes on either side of Mr Pretty's front garden and waited. Gilbert and Daisy on one side; me, February and Charlie on the other. Mr Pretty's house is the only one on the street with a long drive so no one could see us from the road.

Soon, Jacko and his henchmen arrived and crept up to the house. Jacko climbed on Mr Pretty's wheelie bin, whilst the others passed him the worm-filled buckets as he tried to fix them above Pretty's front door. When Mr Pretty opened the door and let everyone in, the buckets would empty all over him.

There was no time to lose. We put our plan into action.

February and me used her Creepy Sound Effects box to play a creaky door opening and an evil witch's laugh. Jacko, Kieran and Abi stopped their giggling and looked around them, but we were all well hidden in the bushes so they couldn't see anything and carried on.

Then we did it again. This time a ghostly 'Oooo' and bats flapping.

'I definitely heard something that time,' whispered Abi.

'Me too. I don't like this, Jacko,' agreed Kieran.

'Oh, don't be complete babies you two, it's just the wind,' snapped Jacko.

Then, from their hiding place, Gilbert and Daisy used Gilbert's fishing rod with a carrot tied to the end of it to tap Kieran on the shoulder – then quickly whizzed it out of sight again.

'Whoa – what was that?' stammered Kieran.

'NOTHING, there's *nothing* there. Stop being a moron and help me fix this bucket in the right place,' hissed Jacko.

The fishing rod struck again, this time without the carrot – just the hook tugging on Kieran's pants before whizzing out of sight again.

'Argh! Was that you!?' screeched Kieran.

'What? No!' scoffed Abi.

'Can you both just . . . shut it . . .' spat Jacko.

But they didn't, and the arguing continued. Turns out, the great thing about bullies is that they don't make for good friends and so it's really easy to break the friendships they do have. After a few more pokes, Jacko exploded at them.

'I'm NOT kidding – WHY do I have to hang out with you two TOTAL KNUCKLEHEADS. Just SHUT UP!' he whisper-shouted.

Kieran and Abi whisper-shouted back at Jacko, told him they never wanted to do this stupid worm stunt anyway and stormed off.

Now it was just Jacko on his own, but he was still determined to fix up the worm buckets. So, we stepped up the noises and the tapping on the shoulder until he was just spinning his head this way and that with a look of sheer terror on his face.

'Very funny, you two!' he hissed into the fading light, with a shaky voice, 'Abi? Kieran? Dudes?'

But he still didn't give up! Instead he returned to the worm buckets.

'We need to do something – scare him more. But how?' I whispered to Charlie in the bush next to me. I wasn't really expecting anything back, apart from maybe a face-five and some crunching noises as he worked his way through yet another tube of Pringles. But, to my surprise, he said, 'I got this.'

Then he produced his creation – a set of telescopic Pringles tubes which, when elongated, were almost two metres long. He quietly angled the long tube up to Jacko's ear as I held my breath.

Then, when the tube was just behind Jacko's ear, he whispered through this end in a super scary creepy voice, 'LEAVE HERE NOW!'

Jacko nearly leapt out of his skin! He turned around but by that time Charlie had retracted the Pringles tubes like a boss and all Jacko could see was darkness.

February sealed the deal by playing one more sound from the bush the other side of him – an evil witch's cackle.

'*ARGHHH!!!!!!*' screamed Jacko, as he leapt off the bin and ran away down the drive. I threw a stone near him, which made him actually jump in fear and race off in the opposite direction to his house – it was so funny!

'We did it!' I whisper-yelled.

February climbed up on the bin and grabbed the two worm buckets.

'Quick,' I said, 'give them to me. I've got an idea! See you all back at The Blockhouse in three minutes.'

I raced back as fast as I could.

When the others joined me at our den they found me sitting in the hammock, smiling and waiting.

'Well, what did you do with the buckets then?' they asked.

I told them to look through the telescope.

They took turns to look and saw Jacko arriving home on his own, opening the door to his den and getting covered in, of course, worms.

'*ARGH!!* ABI AND KIERAN, I'M SO GONNA GET YOU FOR THIS!!!'

Then he ran to his house, trying to shake the worms out of his hair, screaming, 'Mum! Mummy! Mumsy!! Help!'

We all face-fived each other.

'How did you know Jacko wouldn't think it was us?' the others asked. And I told them, 'He just thinks we're a bunch of little dweeby nothings. Only *we* know the truth – that we're actually The Geek Squad, fighting bullies and injustice whenever we find it.'

Then we got down to another game of Spoon Balloon.

Max Crosses the Road

from *The Hodgeheg*
by Dick King-Smith
Illustrated by Ann Kronheimer

*When Max the hedgehog first tried to cross the
road he received a tremendous bang on the head.
But he's determined to find a way. After all,
if humans can do it, why can't hedgehogs?*

THAT EVENING Max waited until he was
sure that Pa was out of the way, in the garden
of Number 5B. The people in 5A always put
out bread and milk for Max's family, but the
people in 5B often provided something much
better for their hedgehogs –
tinned dog food.

Every evening, Pa
crept through the
dividing hedge to see
if he could nick a

saucerful of Munchimeat before his neighbour woke from the day's sleep.

'Ma,' said Max, 'I'm walking for a go.'

Ma was quick at translating by now.

'Did Pa say you could go?' she said.

'No,' said Max, 'but he couldn't say I didn't,' and before Ma could do anything he trotted off along the garden path.

'Oh, Max!' called Ma. 'Are you sure you'll be all right?'

'Yes, of course,' said Max. 'I'll be quite KO.'

Once outside the garden gate he turned left and set off up the road, in the opposite direction to his previous effort. By now he was used to the noise and the brightness, and confident that he was safe from traffic as long as he did not step down into the road. When a human passed, he stood still. The creatures did not notice you, he found, if you did not move.

He trotted on, past the garden of Number 9A with its widow and six kids, until the row of houses ended and a high factory wall began, so high that he would not have been able to read the notice on it beside the factory entrance: Max Speed 5 mph it said.

Max kept going (a good deal more slowly than

this), and then suddenly, once again, he saw not far ahead what he was seeking. Again, there were people crossing the street!

This time they did not go in ones and twos at random, but waited all together and then, at some signal he supposed, crossed at the same time. Max drew nearer, until he could hear at intervals a high, rapid peep-peep-peeping noise, at the sound of which the traffic stopped and the people walked over in safety.

Creeping closer still, tight up against the wall, he finally reached the crossing-place, and now he could see this new magic method. The bunch of humans stood and watched, just above their heads, a picture of a little red man standing quite still. The people stood quite still. Then suddenly the little red man disappeared and underneath him there was a picture of a little green man, walking, swinging his arms. The people walked, swinging their arms, while the high, rapid peep-peep-peeping noise warned the traffic not to move.

Max sat and watched for quite a long time, fascinated by the red man and the green man. He rather wished they could have been a red hedgehog and a green hedgehog, but that was

not really important, as long as hedgehogs could cross here safely. That was all he had to prove, and the sooner the better.

He edged forward, until he was just behind the waiting humans, and watched tensely for the little green man to walk.

What Max had not bargained for, when the bunch of people moved off at the peep-peep-peeping of the little green man, was that another bunch would be coming towards him from the other side of the street. So that when he was about halfway across, hurrying along at the heels of one crowd, he was suddenly confronted by another. He dodged about in a forest of legs, in great danger of being stepped on. No one seemed to notice his small shape and, indeed, he was kicked by a large foot and rolled backwards.

Picking himself up, he looked across and found to his horror that the green man was gone and the red man had reappeared. Frantically, Max ran on as the traffic began to move, and reached the far side just in front of a great wheel that almost brushed his backside. The shock of so narrow an escape made him roll up, and for some time he lay in the gutter whilst above his head the humans stepped on to or off the pavement and the noisy green man and the silent red man lit up in turn.

After a while there seemed to be fewer people about, and Max uncurled and climbed over the kerb. He turned right and set off in the direction of home. How to re-cross the street was, something he had not yet worked out, but in his experience neither striped bits nor red and green men were the answer.

As usual he kept close to the wall at the inner edge of the pavement, a wall that presently gave place to iron railings. These were wide enough apart for even the largest hedgehog to pass between. Max slipped through. In the light of a full moon he could see before him a wide stretch of grass and he ran across it until the noise and stink of the traffic were left behind.

'Am I where?' said Max, looking round him. His nose told him of the scent of flowers (in the Ornamental Gardens), his eyes told him of a strange-shaped building (the Bandstand), and his ears told him of the sound of splashing water (as the fountain spouted endlessly in the Lily Pond). Of course! This was the place that Pa had told them all about! This was the Park!

'Hip, hip, roohay!' cried Max to the moon, and away he ran.

For the next few hours, he trotted busily about the Park, shoving his snout into everything. Like most children, he was not only nosy but noisy too, and at the sound of his coming the mice scuttled under the Bandstand, the snakes slid away through the Ornamental Gardens and the frogs plopped into the safe depths of the Lily Pond. Max caught nothing.

At last he began to feel rather tired and to think how nice it would be to go home to bed. But which way was home?

Max considered this, and came to the unhappy conclusion that he was lost. Just then he saw, not far away, a hedgehog crossing the path, a large hedgehog, a Pa-sized hedgehog! What luck! Pa had crossed the street to find him! He ran forward, but when he reached the animal he found it was a complete stranger.

'Oh,' said Max, 'I peg your bardon. I thought you were a different hodgeheg.'

The stranger looked curiously at him. 'Are you feeling all right?' he said.

'Yes, thanks,' said Max. 'Trouble is, I go to want home. But I won't know the day.'

'You mean . . . you don't know the way?'

'Yes.'

'Well, where do you live?' asked the strange hedgehog.

'Number 5A.'

'Indeed? Well now, listen carefully, young fellow. Go up this path – it will take you back to the street – and a little way along you'll see a strange sort of house that humans use. It's a tall house, just big enough for one human to stand up in, and it has windows on three sides and it's bright red. If you cross there, you'll fetch up right by your own front gate. OK?'

'KO,' said Max, 'and thanks.'

As soon as he was through the Park railings, he saw the tall, red house. He trotted up close to it. It was lit up, and sure enough there was a human inside it. He was holding something to his ear and Max could see that his lips were moving. How odd, thought Max, moving very close now, he's standing in there talking to himself!

At that instant the man put down the receiver and pushed open the door of the telephone booth, a door designed to clear the pavement by about an inch, the perfect height for giving an inquisitive young hedgehog – for the second time in his short life – a tremendous bang on the head . . .

Meet the Bolds

from *The Bolds* by Julian Clary

Illustrated by David Roberts

*The Bolds live in an ordinary house in an
ordinary street – but they are far from
an ordinary family.*

TELLING LIES is NEVER a good idea. I
once told my friends that I was a sausage
roll. I really, definitely was, I said. When they
finally believed me, they squirted me with tomato
ketchup and bit me on the leg.

'Stop it!' I had to shout in the end. 'I'm not a
sausage roll – I am a **human being!**'

That taught me a lesson, I can tell you. I don't
tell lies any more. Ever.

So believe me when I say that the story I am
going to tell you is ABSOLUTELY TRUE. It's

important that you know and understand this, because it is quite an extraordinary story. And funny. Funny peculiar. Very funny peculiar, in fact.

But true. Every word.

The first thing you need to understand before I begin this story is that for some reason human beings have grown rather full of themselves over the years. They now suppose that they are far cleverer than all other living creatures.

This is a mistake. Just because humans can read and write and use knives and forks and computers, they think they are better than other animals. How stupid! Did you know that a squirrel can hide ten thousand nuts in the woods and remember where every single one of them is hidden? Well, I ask you: could you remember where you'd put ten thousand nuts?

Frogs can sleep with their eyes open. Can you?

A cat can lick its own bottom! How clever is that?

The truth is that animals are just as clever as people, but clever in different ways. Animals think people are the stupid ones sometimes.

Next time you pass a field of sheep, stop and look: they will stare back at you with a steady, sympathetic gaze. You might even see them shake their heads if you look closely – amused that we need to wear jumpers and coats made out of wool

that grows perfectly naturally on their backs. What a silly business!

But anyway, back to my story. It begins ten years ago, far away in Africa. Africa, as you may know from photographs and television programmes, is a very hot and beautiful place. There are forests and bush and vast open plains where lots of wild animals live – lions and elephants and giraffes. There are brightly coloured birds that live in the trees, monkeys and gorillas, lizards, hyenas, porcupines and buffaloes. The place is teeming with life of every size and shape you can imagine.

And in Africa, let me tell you, the wild animals are also very clever. They watch human beings and chuckle to themselves. 'Fancy going around cooped up in air-conditioned buses and cars and eating boring cooked food! Humans all look so uncomfortable!

'We so-called "wild" animals wander around freely,' they say to each other. 'Breathing the fresh air and eating fresh food that we catch or pick or graze for ourselves. Far better, in our humble opinion!'

Which lifestyle seems nicer to you?

All the animals in Africa know that the cleverest among them are the hyenas. They aren't the fastest or fiercest, or – let's face it – the most beautiful, but they are smart and determined and work together to get what they want. They are very good at scavenging too.

But the thing hyenas do best, and which drives all the other animals round the twist, is: they laugh.

In fact, they're known as laughing hyenas. Long, loud shrieks and cackles.

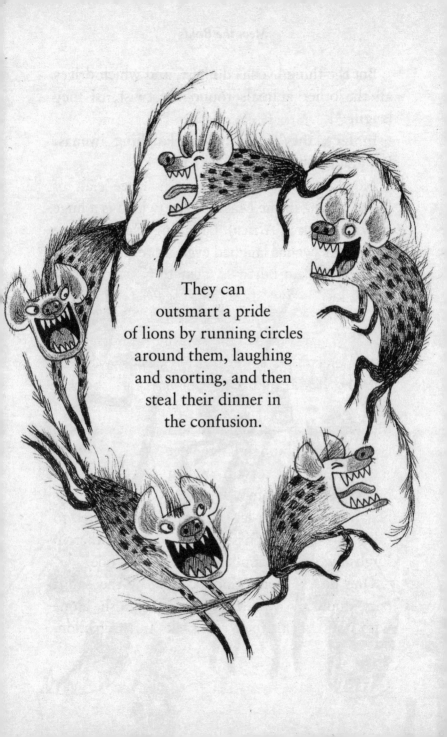

They can
outsmart a pride
of lions by running circles
around them, laughing
and snorting, and then
steal their dinner in
the confusion.

To be honest with you, hyenas are not very popular among the other animals. Birds sing prettily, lions roar impressively, but the incessant laughter of the clever hyenas gives other animals a headache.

Now then. There was once a large clan of hyenas living in the Masai Mara (which is a huge national park in Africa). Laughing hyenas. These particular hyenas laughed even more than most.

They lived in burrows, near to a safari camp, where lots of tourists came to see the animals in their natural environment. Slowly the hyenas became accustomed to their strange visitors. They would creep ever closer to the camp, scavenging leftover food, getting bolder and bolder. Eventually, over time, they began to understand the human way of communicating – they learned to understand human languages.

There were a lot of English visitors at this particular safari camp, so after a while the hyenas began to copy their language and they started to talk. In fact, their first words to each other in English were: 'Cucumber sandwich, anyone?'

One day, a honeymoon couple at the safari park foolishly wandered into the bush alone with nothing but their rucksacks for protection.

Finding the African midday sun too hot for them, they slipped out of their khaki clothes and went for a dip in a pond. Big mistake. Some hungry crocodiles lived there and had those silly humans for lunch.

Cucumber sandwich, anyone?

Two of the English-speaking hyenas, called Spot and Sue, who were actually very much in love, saw what had happened and came to sniff around the discarded items.

'Hey!' said Spot to Sue. 'Come and look at

this!' And he handed her two passports, pulled from one of the bags.

'Well, well!' exclaimed Sue. 'The poor dears

Snap

snap!

Yum

Gulp!

were called Fred and Amelia Bold. May they rest in peace.' The two hyenas stopped for a moment and bowed their heads as they thought about the poor dead humans.

But hyenas are known to be opportunistic creatures, and sure enough, Sue soon had a very daring idea.

'Can you walk on your hind legs, dear?' she asked Spot.

'Then listen,' Sue said excitedly. 'These clothes look like they might fit us. We could put them on and go back to the safari lodge as Fred and Amelia Bold!'

'Then what?' asked Spot, frowning.

'Don't you see?' said Sue. 'This is our way out of here. I've always fancied living in England. Apparently it isn't as hot as Africa and the humans there love queuing. That would make a nice change from always fighting and diving in for scraps of meat here with the rest of the hyena clan. This is our chance for a new life!'

'Oh my!' said Spot with an incredulous laugh. 'That is one BOLD idea! Do you really think we could get away with it?'

'Why not?' said Sue as she continued to look through the dead couple's belongings. 'Look, here

are two plane tickets, a driving licence, house keys, car keys – and our new address: 41 Fairfield Road, Teddington, in Middlesex . . .'

'It does have a nice ring to it,' said Spot, as he slipped into the larger pair of shorts. 'And I must say, these are a perfect fit.'

'Tuck your tail out of the way, for goodness' sake! It's peeking out the bottom of your shorts. That would give the game away.'

Spot laughed. 'Oh, Sue, how I love you!' he said, trying on a large sun hat.

'I'm not Sue any more, remember?' she replied, putting on a posh voice as she buttoned up her khaki shirt. 'From now on, you must call me Amelia. And you, my husband, are Fred! We are Fred and Amelia Bold.'

And with that they both rolled around laughing, before they got up on their hind legs to walk back to the camp and into a new life.

Acknowledgements

The publishers gratefully acknowledge the following, for permission to reproduce copyright material for this anthology.

'Arabel's Birthday' by Joan Aiken from *Mortimer Says Nothing*, published by Puffin Books 1985, text copyright © Joan Aiken 1985; reissued in *More Arabel and Mortimer*, published by Puffin Books 2019, reprinted by permission of Penguin Random House; illustrations copyright © Quentin Blake 1985, 2019, reprinted by permission of Penguin Random House and United Agents. 'Little Badman/Big Trouble' by Humza Arshad and Henry White from *The Invasion of the Killer Aunties,* published by Puffin Books 2018, text copyright © Humza Arshad and Henry White 2018; illustrations copyright © Aleksei Bitskoff 2018, reprinted by permission of Penguin Random House. 'Noble Warrior' by Clare Balding from *The Racehorse Who Wouldn't Gallop*, published by Puffin Books 2017, text copyright © Clare Balding 2017; illustrations copyright © Tony Ross 2017, reprinted by permission of Penguin Random House. 'Meet the Bolds' by Julian Clary from *The*

Meet a troublesome elephant, a lonely lion,
a selfish pirate and many other extraordinary
characters in this exciting collection of short stories.

The
Puffin Book
of STORIES for
5 year
olds

Edited by WENDY COOLING

Perfect to share with five-year-olds.

Meet a greedy monkey, a friendly tiger, a missing
Martian and many other unusual characters
in this lively collection of short stories.

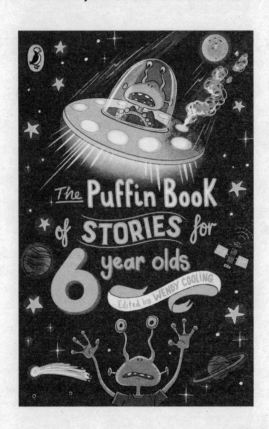

Perfect to share with six-year-olds.

Meet a princess who's bored of fairy tales, a hungry gorilla, a grumbling snowman and many other surprising characters in this timeless collection of short stories.

Perfect to share with seven-year-olds.

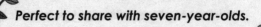

Meet a foolish king, a very bad giant, a boastful fish and the cleanest family ever in this fun-filled collection of short stories.

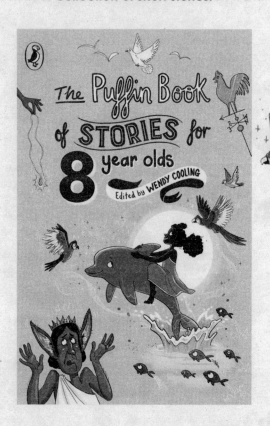

The Puffin Book
of STORIES for
8 year olds
Edited by WENDY COOLING

Perfect to share with eight-year-olds.